Harmony in Bad Taste

Darby Guise

Bear Skin Bob Press

Also by Darby Guise

The Drunk'unn Boat

Harmony in Bad Taste

ISBN 978-1-7775275-3-2

Contents

Hell is a cartoon & heaven is a tea party.

—Judd Quinn

Prologue: ✳

They sat at the same booth as last time near a window. He ordered a grilled cheese, and she ordered a hamburger; an old man and a kid sat across from them. The old man spoke to the kid who feigned interest and pushed his peas towards his potatoes. A popular pharmaceutical ad came on the television, and the old man set off towards the bathroom.

Out of earshot from the dining patrons, the old man sat discarding dislodged stools from his bowels. He pulled a felt-tip pen from his shirt pocket and drew four intersecting lines and wrote the word "asshole" underneath. Next to it, he drew an identical image and wrote the word "universe." He exited the bathroom without washing his hands and stared absentmindedly at the crowd near the booth by the window.

Chapter 1: Gwen

When Gwen was seven, she would sit beside her father and watch the television set. Cartoons were flanked by newsreel footage; bombs curtailed overgrown puppets; consumer jingles flirted with post-punk anthems.

Gwen was a well-spirited child with a sharp wit; her cantankerous style employed subtle degrees of cuteness and developed into a strong means to abate the common authoritative male.

Their television-program odysseys provided an assortment of terrain to work through Gwen's commonplace anxieties, and she attested a divine worship to the channel-surfing thumb of her father. It was his genius, a knack for tone, an intuitive gift employed in the nick of time, crafting a collage of sights and sounds developed from the urges of his fruitless whims.

After being pushed at the water fountain, Gwen walked off and cried in the nook near the gymnasium.

Alone, she sat, huddled in her upstairs bedroom. Arms tightly wound 'round bunched-up knees; thunder belched thick with angst.

Back at school, that bitch Janine, as Gwen would pronounce in her head, hunched forward, the aggressor, throwing heft and bone, a meat engine of pubescent farm girl, attacking the meek—the frail, wide-eyed Gwen—that bitch Janine.

***

The dilettante preacher pontificated about the hunt. He wore an askew grin on a pixelated visage. A man of no more than 40 whose health habits fostered an arrogant concession to decadence. He swung his Winchester rifle onto his camouflaged shoulder; the theatrics showcased a gluttonous underbelly dipping below a snug-fitting shirt. Gwen stewed in anger at the display as her father fumbled with the remote.

Their journey through the sports channels had taken the brunt of Gwen's emotional outpour, and she lashed out at the televised frames, taking no heed of good manners or sentimental trappings.

But Gwen lacked conviction, and her inability to endure anger's delirium rarely allowed its prejudices to take root, and her hateful gaze evolved into a wayward apology and a complimentary nod.

Her fretting was not with them; scapegoats, they were. Miniature victims at the crossroads of an ill-fated remote.

She sat quietly as her father regained control and made his way downward towards the lower 200s. A brief stint of randomized movie networks was fast approaching. A Hail Mary to be run through at a blitz pace. Her eyes welled up in anticipation.

The movie networks offered little in the way of spectacle, and her father's thumb cruised on, a rhythmic rat-tat-tat, drumming through a long succession of missed opportunity and unwanted artifice. Gaining speed. Did he have a destination? A goal? Who knew? Speech was not part of the deal.

Dónde vamos? Oú allons-nous? Onde estamos indo?

Where was this motherfucker going?

***

The next day, Gwen shoved Janine, the onslaught of taunts proved too much on this particular morning.

Janine toppled, submitting to the rigid formality of the public school desks surrounding her fall. Her arm busted in two places, bruised and battered chunks. Both girls stunned, trying to register the event.

"Shit," thought Gwen. "I've really done it."

"There's no pride in abstinence." She read the words which hijacked a corner of Ms. McArthur's desk. Perhaps some child of yesteryear had scribbled it; the blind or aloof receptionist allowed the words to endorse a small nook near its crest: a throwback to youthful anarchism or simply an overlooked bit of juvenile graffiti?

Who was Ms. McArthur? A woman of robust build brandishing a cultivated indifference. She preferred women to men, books to people, narcotics to travel. She showed little ambition and sought to never exceed the bare minimum. She was a satisfactory receptionist, generally well liked, an intermediary among the frivolous office affairs, and a comfort to many, including Gwen.

The principal ushered Gwen into his office and offered a curt yet unassuming nod.

Principal MacWell: Would you like a mint?

... perpetrator, inflictor of pain, demagogue of justice.

She shook her head and declined his offer, silent and confused by the supposed generosity of his gesture. He withdrew and popped two callous-looking mints to the rear of his mouth, jowls jostling to the rhythm of his placid speech, and each took their seat.

By the time Principal MacWell had concluded, Gwen had been administered a wide variety of toxins. Pious and futile attempts to secure a moral framework in which the principal could justify his role, feed his ego, demand a serotonin-based elixir for his rotten soul siphoned from her impulsive deed.

Gwen channeled an agreeable air when faced with such prideful authoritarians, dialing in the intensity to match the megalomania of her foe. A trick to secure footing, ease through the proceedings, minimize damage. She sheepishly nodded at the principal's righteous preaching and underwent her penance as the lunatic raved on for over an hour before her father arrived.

***

COMEDIAN: What's the similarity between a biological parent and an axe murderer?

They both condemn a being to die...

The crowd erupts in laughter but is never pictured, only the sad face of the comic lingers, unable to escape the frame as the applause rise to abnormal sonic heights. Dissonance and dread pierce the soundtrack, intolerable screeching, noises of insanity. His brain is being fucked; damage is being done. He twists in agony, clutches his ears, knocks over the microphone; the sound builds, layers in intensity; he shuffles but cannot escape. It's wormed its way in. It tunnels through his cerebral organ. Terror deepens in his eyes as he stares into the camera, aware of its imminence, praying for it, begging for it... His head bursts, a joyous release; the sound stops, silence; the body performs yet more theatrics, kneels baring the cavity wherefrom a head once stood, comically falls forward—a tour de force—the screen fades to black. Gwen looks over and sees her father, head back, asleep on the couch. He snores, and she clutches the remote—heart pounding; the name of the film is "... or A HIGH DOSE OF TRUTH IS DETRIMENTAL TO SURVIVAL." She has control, a rare occasion. She changes the channel in search of more treasures.

She watches a percussionist. Ass back, chest up, perched like a peacock. End of the page. He flicks his baton forward, unprepared—bored, she moves on.

Next channel, Maybelline... next channel, giant squid... next channel, tits... next channel, Pepsi... next channel, cruiser... next channel... cops.... next... no signal... next... infomercial... next... and on and on and on.

She wakes up still holding the remote, tucked into an oversized armchair, alone, still enveloped in a world without parental consent. She walks the halls, sees her father asleep, head down. He opens his eyes: the spell breaks.

Father: Breakfast?

She shakes her head, twists the whole of her vertebral column, exaggerating the gesture. He smiles for effect.

He lights another cigarette and waves goodbye. She exits the front door and narrowly catches the school bus.

Off-balanced by the abnormalities of the previous day, the bus ride takes on a peculiar air. She sits beside Steph, usual spot, and sighs at her best friend's befuddled musings.

School.

Gwen sits at her desk; Ms. Stevenson writes numerical values in large font on the chalkboard. The conditions are primed, an unruly education is poised to begin; she's set adrift, relaxed, events unfurl, squabbles resurface. This is life, or so she thinks, briefly, but the timeline moves on; a locomotion of sensations aggregated to a fixed point, epitomized in a tone, pluralize to a beat.

Janine enters; Gwen's daydreams find an abrupt end. The bully's arm is in a cast, and there's a slight expression of shame exposed across her brow. She takes her seat, three behind Gwen. No words are exchanged between the pair, Ms. Stevenson continues on. Gwen's heart beats fast, but the presiding forty-five minutes of monotony allow it to regain composure before the bell rings, and the kids are dismissed for recess.

She spots her near the tire house. Is this it? The final showdown? Good against evil? David against Goliath? But who's Goliath? She, Gwen, has the upper hand. A quarter of Janine's limbs are immobilized. Is she the bully?

No...

She should end it now—finish it—crush her enemy. Add shame to the physical injury. Pour salt on the wound. Laugh at the big girl's miscalculations of the little mademoiselle's fury. Wouldn't it be the right thing to do? End the conflict. Decapitate the Hydra. Save the next victim... for posterity!

But then she catches a glimpse of an unknown object whirl by. An ancient curiosity embedded in the fiber of her being shifts her focus left. Three boys and a hill. One stands on top, two glued to its base. The uppermost one cocks his head to the left and then to the right. He's confused. His vantage point conceals the two minions below, each cowering, covering their mouths, stifling the laughter, prone to secrecy.

And then it's time. Arise. One of the minions hops to his feet, leans back, a swift maneuver, and fires a stone at the boy above. It stays the course, and the resounding cry—feeble and helpless—reiterates the success of the throw. The boy on top topples, the minions rise, and their laughter echoes. They walk up the hill towards their fallen comrade, whose cries morph into a sordid chuckle: half frenzied pain, half morbid relief.

"So, this is how boys play," mutters Gwen. "What utter stupidity."

The three boys sit on the hilltop, tension relieved. Gwen's focus rearranged by the episode, she seeks out her pal Steph to relay the ordeal, gossip about the tomfoolery.

As she walks away, back facing Janine, she hears one of the boys yell, "Right in the *dink*... I got him right in the dink!"

Chapter 2: Johnny

Corralled into the gymnasium—short stock—between the ages of 6 and 11. Squads of rectangles waiting for the addressing party to begin. John is 7, has to pee, downed two juice boxes at recess; head honcho, Ms. McGregor, would probably let him, irritable type though, presumable sneers during their parley, before and if she grants him the pissing privilege. He decides against it, tries to redirect his attention. "What the hell are we *here* for?"

A man, mid-forties, is standing, center stage, below the stage, near a mic, ground floor. John hears the fan of an overhead projector hiss, and the AV crowd pushes a button, and an image strikes a pose on the adjacent wall next to a cartoon werewolf—the school's mascot, Bernard.

"Hello, thank you for joining me today. I'm..."

John notices his error right away. He overestimated the size of his prepubescent bladder. Discomfort and physical uneasiness are of primary concern.

"*Goddammit!*" It's too late; he knows it. Sit and deal. His legs are crossed, one hand nonchalantly close to his package, an indicator, just in case there's boilover, and he has to make a run for it.

"Sorry, Ms. McGregor, stream's a flowing, to hell with you." She'll understand in hindsight. Take pity on the poor fool.

"What the hell is he blabbering on about anyway?"

The man marks the acetate; the kids stare; a grotesque dance of light masquerades as a hand. Soft chatter and a sense of hushed ritual, a dim excitement scatters amongst them. John clutches his privates who've since been promoted to defensive backs in a double-Dutch effort to contain the spill, but it's no use...

***

Sweet relief. Piss unloads in yellow tinges against the porcelain backdrop. He made it... mostly, minor damage. Considering the alternatives, he thanks his lucky stars.

He basks in physical delight, flares his nostrils, and opens them to the evocative odor.

He returns to the gymnasium, junky-level euphoria pre-scribes an aura around him. He sits in the back, outside the pack, with a couple of stray teachers who snicker in the darkness. He looks to the overhead and sees the score.

Car accident, cancer, cerebral hemorrhaging, murder, suicide, lung carcinoma, diabetes, drugs, gastrointestinal disorders, and the list goes on. Each cause matched to a number tallied together with the sum reaching 386 and the words "total" and "students" thrown in for good measure.

The speaker has bred national statistics with enrollment records and created a death-row transvestite hocking a horoscope of doom, branding infantile brains with questions the likes of: "Well, who survives, then?" which gives rise to the demon, smacking bloodstained lips, who whispers, "No one." At least that's the show playing in John's head.

"Christ almighty!" He's upset and startled at the realization, a sudden attestation to the unavoidable failure etched across the room. He feels abandoned but isn't quite sure by whom.

John finds out later that the overzealous spectacle was a no-smoking assembly. Not-so-subtle tremors are still being felt, invoking an urge to perform rudimentary mental math on schoolyard soccer girls, learning the dire secret that lies beyond statistical analysis: if Lisa doesn't die in a car crash, surely Joan or Judy will. It's all in the numbers. The cold, hard unavoidable numbers.

So spoke John, or the voice of John, in the head of John, who shunned this arbitrary chatter with newfound zeal and gusto and plunged headlong into study and sport. This providing the overarching fuel for his teens and twenties, before the thought child, born this very day, awoke to unleash agony and torment on the poor fella. And so our hero waits out the next two decades, a bon vivant and a decadent young man, awaiting his union with the eventual.

***

Written by a 9th grader on the boys' washroom wall:
/Bored/Tired/Slighted/Wronged/Gorged/Sleeping/Right/ Wrong/Nigger/Nazi/Gook/Whore/Dyke/Cunt/Wop/Roar/H ick/Deadbeat/Loser/Freak/Metalhead/Muslim/Martyr/Gree k/Bored/Tired/Slighted/Wronged/Gorged/Sleeping/Right/ Wrong/Nietzsche/Naughty/Gook/Whore/Dick/Cunt/Wasp/ Roar/Hick/Deadbeat/Loser/Freak/Fag/Muslim/Martyr/Gee k/Bored/Tired/Slaughtered/Wronged/Gorged/Weeping/Rig ht/Wrong/Nigger/Nazi/Gook/Whore/Dyke/Cunt/Wop/Roar

/Hick/Deadbeat/Loser/Freak/Metalhead/Muslim/Martyr/G
reek/Bored/Tired/Slighted/Wronged/Gorged/Sleeping/
Right/Wrong/

Chapter 3: Richard

The puck crosses center ice; Jacque's head swivels back; a shoulder wedges perpendicular and fractures Louis' jaw.

Richard's will spoke in fragmented form and concocts an idea, "Skate left... yes, yes... skate left..."

He plucks the puck from a cross-ice saucer pass meant for Laurence. He caresses it, side to side, and heads for the net.

He cuts hard, leans left, shoots—a triumphant uproar overtakes the crowd. He lifts his arms in celebration, a flood of endorphins rush his middle-class mind.

Stiff hips and battered vertebrae are the trophies of the day. Pride evaporates as paternal instincts resurface one step outside the dressing room. Men march out, hockey bags slung over sunken shoulders. Wives hold toddlers who communicate in hard *g*'s and repetitive vowels. "Gooooo," says one. "Gaaaaa," says the other.

They exit the arena parking lot and take a left on Jeremiah Lane. A billboard reads, "Everyone loves a good grimace."

They take sips from thermal mugs whose antidotes hold equal parts coffee and malt liquor.

The snow continues its hypnotic descent. The Sirens of Winter act as ephemeral guardians against the virtues of road safety, swaying drivers left when they should go right.

He drops her off at her country abode, a long driveway with a barbed fence. Christmas lights illuminate past memories, familial ties, an insulated haven safeguarded by two howling Rottweilers.

He curves the bend, retraces his path, emerges, tires skidding, and ratchets up the volume knob. There's no indication of the horizon, just ceaseless darkness echoed above and below.

Richard pulls a cigarette from his shirt pocket and nestles it where his lateral incisor used to be; a slap shot some years back had forced him to reappraise his looks, eschewing words like handsome and enamel-y endowed.

He grows weary of the visual monotony. The highway offers rhythm but little in the realm of aesthetic diversity.

It's a singular moment, hind legs in headlights—a revolting crash, an intrusive jerk. The cerebral lights cut to black.

When he comes to, he registers an acrid smell. He tries to open his eyes; in accordance with the command, only the left abides. The right rewires the circuit south. His jaw goes slack.

He tongues at the fag still lodged in place and sets it in motion. It somersaults along his jacket.

***

The beast is lopped in a series of rogue geometric abnormalities, oozing through shards of disfigured glass and jagged metals, pulsating, a live dissection. The twisted display is an abomination to even the foulest of obscenities, playing along to the whimsical aestheticism of some monstrous deity; its grotesque form now bastardized to an apoplectic smear along the roadway.

He's about to pass out. The final frames further the insult as Richard's head falls forward, noting the beast's final act of contrition, a unifying gesture. Bone and viscera mingle with lacerated musculature upon the vinyl interior and the beast's hoof jets through Richard's left shin. The visuals alter the balance in favor of the abyss, and his eyes roll back, and the lights dim.

He dreams of a man in a blue suit. He speaks in incomprehensible blurbs that annoy Richard no end. As the man's speech dives in a diminuendo, Richard notices a shallow growl coming from the fringe of his *discorso*, communicating a lost meaning, a meanderer of intent. Richard hurries to decrypt the code as the volume reduces beyond his audible range. Times up. He senses that the dream will end soon as structural norms dictate it will, but the dream continues to linger on with both men rooted in silence, stuck in nothingness. Ennui takes hold of him, and he sits down. Eventually, he wakes up.

Richard awakens to find himself prisoner to an odd visual abstraction. Uncertain its origin, he remembers the beast and the accident and pieces the puzzle together as best he can. Unable to move, he looks at the grizzled contusion before his eyes. Remnants of the mighty beast deformed in pictorial dyslexia.

Something bubbles from an unknown orifice. The beast is not dead. It lets out a symphony of hard-boiled harmonics. Gurgles and spits, gurgles and spits. Richard tries to do the same. Communicate. He can't tell whether his efforts are in vain, if messages are being sent or received. He passes out...

It's entirely black; his mind feels compressed, immobile; his body's weightless or nonexistent; an emotion approaches, an anticipatory feeling; it loiters, never reaching its climactic height, inches away, prolonged ad infinitum...

And then something nears... an interruption... a formal oddity... symbolic, significant... its fanged limbs contort, sending out disarraying signals of mental molestation. Richard can no longer hold on to the joyous brink of anticipatory bliss. He begins to convulse, bubbling in dysmorphic agony. He's unhinged; sensations develop; a psyche is born. He's squeezed, suctioned, thrust out, blinded and cold. He communicates his dissatisfaction: wails and cries, wails and cries. He's cradled. Embraced. He calms down. Gurgles and spits. Gooooos and gaaaaas...

"Christ," he thinks, "this again."

***

Poem written on the arena wall:
Praise be to God, whomever Ye may be,
Praise be to Allah and Mephistopheles,
And randomness and will,
To chaos and subjugation,
And calculated probability.

To Judy and wellness,
And all that is sublime.
To salvation and damnation,
And labyrinthian lies.

Another one written near the toilet:
/fool/foe/harlequin/fan/
follower/evildoer/fanatic/plan/
racist/mongrel/primitive/youth/
volatile/unfeeling/insurgent/untruth/
disgust/hatred/retribution/rebirth/
mother/father/Oedipus/cursed/

Chapter 4: _____

He described himself as neither pessimist nor stoic, but he certainly lived among them, or near them, on a neighboring rock, and he interpreted his philosophy through a lens most would have characterized as insane. But he was also someone who liked to have fun (fun is the gun, he'd say… or was it fun is the sun?), even though a darkness always loomed thick upon his shoulders or beneath his brow, and he could never entirely rid himself of it or dispel it or even pretend it didn't accompany him everywhere he went. At least that was the abbreviated form as to how he would have described himself if anyone had cared to ask.

Some said his soul was the great vaginal abyss or a riptide of madness at its very best.

"Alleviate my error through the good grace of your infallible reason, you *heinous* little prick. Explain at once!" said the old woman to our hapless hero.

And his response: "I plan on shitting in the world's mouth

and duct-taping its mouth shut."

Like anyone who'd achieved greatness, he'd given up the need to be understood long ago.

He created his own antidote to the venom and subdued the poison coursing through his veins—at least for the time being.

And thus began the brouhaha or, as some called it, the donnybrook...

***

He was a born superhero, and on January 5th, 1998, he awoke and snorted the final remnants of leftover cocaine from the top of his rustic dresser. A pharmacopeia blitz had ensued the night prior with his fellow caped crusaders, lounging and snorting after a successful night of heroic feats, squashing the tyrannical plans of the evil urban mongrels rising from the city's darkened underbelly. He would need the added buzz of illicit drugs to make it through his morning rounds, errands which included a visit to the local haberdashery to outfit his new costume with shiny metallic buttons.

He locked up the house and deposited the key in his left breast pocket with a gentle movement from his red right hand.

"I've spent some of my best days entirely alone and some of my worst in the company of homicidal, narcissistic, debauched, treacherous, conniving, vampiric, cyanide-loving and acid-throwin', inbred, lynch-mobbing, groupthinkin', pseudo–'nice and modern,' well-adjusted and typically ordinary people."

The assumption that things are new because they're repackaged... or that normal or stable even exists—cycles and fashions and word games.

To beautiful failures above mediocre successes, and to dim excitement above bright exuberance, and to the scared stiff above the bravely stupid, and to their counterpoints and opposites and equals. May their balance find their intensity and prosper among the light as well as the dark.

—Superhero prayer

A narrative was another word for a map, and an artist was another word for cartographer, and everyone was a caricature of someone else he knew.

And when they asked him what he thought of the current state of affairs, he said, "Forget it, Jake. It's Chinatown."

When he watched TV, he saw the unimaginative yearnings of the masses. A masquerade of dull wishes and phantom desires, a hocus-pocus game of dress-up, performed and corrupted from the early days of their youth. A primitive game played by earnest hypocrites, all of whom desired the most extravagant and deplorable of fantasies, none more truly than our beautiful and sad hero, the modern Bacchus, the caped jackass himself, _____.

The robber pointed his pistol at _____, who in turn broke the perp's nose and dislocated his jaw. He exhumed a stylish assortment of seldom-used kicks that he'd learned in the Alps while training under his master, ____*____*____. This caused significant trauma to the perpetrator's iliac crest and crippled him for months and permanently affected his gait. He would often be ridiculed in later years for the way he walked, this incident irrevocably shattering his self-image.

The destroyer wields the ultimate weapon and lives in the sanctity of gloom and ridiculousness. This requires a perilous journey undertaken by only the most brave and foolish sorts. Long and hard is their way, hell-bent on its own destruction; alone, they wander. Doomed from the get-go, although it was the only real journey—even though it was an imaginative one—and yet those who took it, few in number, could do nothing to either advance or negate its forward momentum. Submissive to its whims, downward they fell, crushed and waiting until they were called upon to rise, shedding the skin of their former selves, embracing the hope of a new idea, fusing old worn-out symbols, and crafting immutable armors against the decay of the day; they outfit and assemble, sharpening their weapons, their icons of destruction, and seek to produce a tremor of fear or a frightful shift in the cosmic game. Aware of its futility, its inevitable and probable failure, they are nonetheless compelled. They recede into the earth, waiting patiently for the necessary ingredients—for the very utterance from God—or whichever deity or chemical aberration dislodged the idea. Watchdogs, superheroes, and villains lie buried, hoping to rise again under the guise and guidance of something more enduring and more dangerous and, perhaps, more beautiful.

He thought that maybe by trying to destroy the world, he'd somehow save it. This absurdity stood the test of time and became the core of his philosophy, embedding itself deep under a mound of nonsense and horseshit in the crevices of his rotting brain. Shifting the tide from hero to supervillain, he molded his persona and emerges... tires skidding, and ratchets up the volume knob...

"And Christ," he thinks, "one more time from the beginning."

Chapter 5: Joyce

It stood on the edge of town, perched on a hilltop, a seldom-visited place for most folks, a graveyard of hodgepodge goods, illegitimate brand names, and half-empty shelves.

Joyce walks in, grabs a cart and heads down the dairy aisle, passing vertebrates gnashing imaginary teeth, showcasing Mesozoic skinfolds and pockmarked cheeks. She gets a whiff of urine as she passes an old woman who signals colloquial clichés to each passerby. She is one among many in a sea of middle-aged perms and elderly tanning beds.

He sits alone, cutting the loin of lamb, thick slices.

Dim light pours putrid orange over perishable goods. A tungsten glow bears down on naked produce, nullifying pre-conceived notions of color and creed, leaving all aggrieved, except, of course, the orange ones.

(In Russian accent)

He is butcher, Jason, forty-five years old, divorced. Spry hairs sprout from collar neck. Pouty face. Elongated jaw. Protruding chin. Muttonchops.

She walks towards the meat counter.

He sees her coming, and he saws the meat in a rhythmic fashion, no pauses; he hopes she notes the musicality of his performance, which, of course, she does.

Joyce is wet and lambasts her biological quirk, an odd fetishism prone to lubrication in the presence of raw meat.

"Carnal longings? Where does this come from? And why does it have to happen to me?" A voice from within responds, "Universal mysteries," and Joyce wonders why the voice is identifiably male and not without hints of her father's intonation. "Universal mysteries," the words echo again, this time from the vocal cavity of what seems to be that of an eight-year-old girl.

"Strange," mutters Joyce in full earshot of the butcher who, for one reason or another, hears "orange" and, in his confusion, mutters, "You're a mystery," and she hears "universal mysteries," and their eyes fix and neither can comprehend why they can't break from the other's gaze.

A swelling penis, a quivering vagina, and markedly odd confusion: these are the ingredients lending themselves to the present scenario.

***

Jason: How can I help you?

She signals towards him with a crooked, dainty *doigt*—points her finger in the vicinity of his lap.

After a brief pause, she adds...

Joyce: What kind of meat are you cutting?

Jason's overeagerness to deliver a satisfactory response prompts him to divulge a glorious mess of syllables containing no rightful answer. He is muted by embarrassment and tries his hand at a redemptive gesture, something to right his wrong, win back her confidence through graceful physicality. He forgets he's holding a knife.

The knife rises fast; blood separates from its serrated edge and escapes headlong over the counter. Joyce takes two splotches in the chest, one in the arm, a smack to the left cheek below the orbital cavity, and a buckshot—two inches thick—spread across her left eyebrow.

Each is stunned. Jason stands; his erection marks a noticeable outline in his trousers. He drops the knife. "Bam," says the concrete floor.

The spewed discharge has caused Joyce's vagina to assert itself even further, beyond good taste and polite sociability, increasing to the point of overflow.

She comes, hands pressed firmly against rattled sex organ. She tries to downplay the pleasurable gyrations, wayward eyes upon her and all, strangers gawking in the midst of her bloody plight.

Jason: I'm so sorry.

Joyce: It's okay.

As if by impulse, she relinquishes her tongue and mops up a dollop of blood from her upper lip. It tastes of iron, and residual particles linger over her right cuspid. This, however, goes unnoticed by Jason whose concerns lie elsewhere.

She wipes her face, smears the blood, blends it to her pigment—a natural rouge sheen. He hands her a napkin; she blots, and he comes back, this time, holding a moistened tissue, for ultimate removal. He continues to apologize; his erect penis pressed to the frozen back of the display case, shielding it from view, a cooling antidote.

He hands her the meat, averts his gaze, and offers a polite, albeit embarrassed, nod.

She exits stage right.

The episode will linger in Jason's mind for some time. Unconscious motifs ride coattails alongside replayed mental jargon. The modus operandi attests to the richness of the episode, however incomplete and ignorant, calling it voluptuous and ripe, symbolic and plentiful; a perfect phantom cocktail when paired with Jason's distinguished psyche.

Maya... chimera... the whole goddamned kit and caboodle... emotional wasteland... *día de los locos*...

He builds up the storyline, fills in the blanks, masturbates furiously to the tale; unconditional surrender to the depravity, at least for the couple of minutes required to get the job done, in solitude, of course, a momentary furlough with a negligible cleanup. "Could this be love?"

Joyce, on the other hand, forgets or represses the episode (who can honestly tell the difference) and fertilizes her pride with minor accomplishments won throughout the day. Regular binges of daytime television are enough to keep the wheels from digging too deep... God bless her beautiful soul.

(She had that wise blood.)

Chapter 6: George

He just didn't want to be at the beck and call of anyone's mood anymore, not even his own. A perverse dexterity had accompanied his nausea from the onset, dismantling any attempt he ever made toward grandeur. He was alone in a world that didn't want him, or so he felt, and this perversion enabled a clarity of vision unsung in common songs. A lullaby for mountaintops, a silent soliloquy.

***

George sees her across the roadway and begins to dart through heavy traffic. His sneakers crunch a quintet of cockroaches, and an ambulance ejects a rage-stricken paramedic, torso deep, shaking a half-eaten slice of pizza from the passenger-side window; it zooms by, and pedestrian George moseys on, the undaunted jaywalker. He neither hears nor sees any of the miasmic happenings devouring his journey, for in front, behold, his girl, the symbol of love, his love, a desperate love, a figure to preclude all cosmic dangers.

She is 5′2″, brunette, tanned skin with nipples the size of nickels. They stand out to him, whisper secrets, perched on golden mounds, confessionals pointed slightly skyward. A biology of perfection, a genealogy of genius, the culmination of aesthetic ideals snug in black leggings and a loose-knit shirt.

Her name is Bess, blue-eyed Betsy; they met at the café, bumping elbows, offering up swift glances, sensual exchanges, feigned laughter, chitchat and the like—awkward first date, delightful first fuck, a two-month sojourn, a romantic vehicle careening towards an impasse destined for catastrophe.

Bess,
the embodiment of balance,
the skillful manipulator,
the goddess of the rebuke,
the prime composer,
the articulator of tenderness,
a sublime ballet of beauty,
the mother and the wench,
the dominator of cruelty.

Now George,
Georgie, old boy,
fate's bastard kin,
a reserve of negligence,
a lackadaisical warrior,
a trespasser,
a stillborn,
a connoisseur of the fuck,
he lies near the throne of genius,

surviving beyond empathy and envy,
a gentle soul,
the lapdog of luck.

... But, for the moment, George is outside himself. Enchanted by the damsel, he seeks no further validation than her own. She is, after all, a goddess—a harrowing nymph, a flowering of grace; he submits to her willfully, echoing a simple desire deep in the depths of many men...

the basis of a dire weakness,
yet perhaps the noblest of apocalyptic quests,
the weeping lily,
the harbinger of the fall,
a longing to be devoured
by the most beautiful creature of them all.

He looks at her across the table, and she licks her lips, imparting a slimy display of texture to their glossy curvature. She is immersed in her own image... again; navigating the depths of her reflected image off the candlelit silverware, she doesn't notice him and jiggles her jaw about—sucking in her cheeks—endowing herself with coquettish fancy, unaware of his mounting anxiety. She will not eat him; he is too meek, too weak, too affable. He is ignorable and unwilling to be cruel. She will discard him soon enough, and his pain will be excruciating. Thus falls the dagger of love's disdain.

He is ejected from the restaurant for having spat at the maître d'. All desires are hell-bent on his moral and physical self-destruction.

"When will this stop?"

He is unaware that "this" is the symphony, the reason, the rhythm, the tonal DNA, written in space, conducted through the annals, the infernal beat of the incurable sickness.

(Bess' profundity was marked by an expertise in superficiality with an intellect to destroy.)

There was nothing necessary to say, nothing worthy to up-hold, nothing safe to be supporting; it was all ill devised and, therefore, ill defined. George knew this, and all at once, the words struck deep, dismantling the paralysis of affection that had coiled itself around his eyes like blinders.

A life lived well was lived for an audience of one: an inert schizophrenic with peculiar tastes and a violent whimsy—the *anima*.

The thought brought George to a dead stop, and Betsy walked on, continuing to chatter to the invisible specter of where she supposed George to be, only coming to terms with his sudden disappearance ten or twelve paces thereafter.

The feeling was strange and sifted through drunken stupor and emotional neglect; the resulting stew prompted an imaginary séance forecasting what was sure to be. George saw himself in the throes of passion, kissing Betsy, caressing her lavish contours, sampling the suppleness of her flesh. She moaned and ached, arched and sighed, and all at once, he came to the deafening rush of chemical prestige; the exodus of semen splattered across her stomach.

Common ethics are often petty, and so Betsy (being a being above the mean) mopped up the residue of George's excess and lit a cigarette and, sparse as her actions were, showcased her complete and utter disregard for him.

Neither in anger nor in ecstasy was her postcoital dance ever more vehement than here, when he supposed she would abide and surrender to his mystique. Was there not a more appropriate time in which a lover could yield, even modestly, than after the throes of love? He supposed not, and with this answer came the feeling, and with the feeling came his return, and with his return came the vomit, and he doubled over and puked in the gutter as Bess watched ten or twelve paces yonder.

He was really nice and therefore had really fucked-up insides.

Those she liked best liked her least.

He contented himself smiling at the madness of it all.

She understood despair but only on a superficial level.

The End.

And as the great poet said, "*Me retracto de todo lo dicho.*"

For now, I am drunk on love, and for the moment, time's weight ceases to be a burden.

I take it all back. I am drunk, and life is beautiful, or put another way, love is the crack.

Chapter 7: The Centipede

It started out in an odd fashion, begot by circumstances outside its usual orbit. Was it deaf to the mutations beyond its sensory range? Probably, but who really knows?

He sees it on the wall. A goddamn centipede, sprawled; its spread elongated beyond the usual predicted measures. It fawns over its existence and sets about in a semi-circular jive upwards, along taupe-painted contours and bric-a-brac and miscellaneous paraphernalia.

"I renounce all expectation in favor of the daring dance. I wallow in a hollow of a creeping, sorry sack. I am God of the meaningless with meningitis of the spine. The supine Queen of Cataracts with a blank prescription for the benign."
—the centipede

He's comatose on the couch with a slack jaw and supinated palms; even the appearance of the centipede doesn't rouse more than nominal interest in our dilapidated hero.

He is droll in the worst sort of way.

"Scepter of my sphincter,
Repetitious ritual rite,
Crowing bowels of congress,
A comet sings within the night,
'Tis dark amongst you mortals,
Every dog shall have its day,
Spoke the scepter of my sphincter,
Liturgical *clin d'oeil* of cliché."
—the centipede

He contemplates violent behavior momentarily, but the crutch of the couch crucifixion nullifies expedient action beyond limited vocal commands issued from a hoarse, smoke-stained larynx falling upon presumably deaf arthropod sensory cells.

"surfing fly,
cannibalistic eye,
degenerative growth,
outpour of sap,
sentimental crap,
veer left,
upon hardened terrain,
unspoken-for multitudes,
diseases for the gods,
ripe for production,
continue straight,
towards the aborted sound,
smile, my love,
we're harvest bound."
—the centipede

The nocturnal nautilus spirals and devours its prey. The centipede has found a grounded fly and with exacting severity has performed a discombobulating disembowelment, munching away will and limb in a curled, cockeyed contortion. The grotesque dance jolts John's guts awake.

He leans forward, bright-eyed and bushy-tailed, subservient to the gluttonous beauty taking place before his occipital lobe. He watches the centipede whose predatory disposition gives way to lethargic merriment; its gorged, worm-like corpus working overtime to bend and distort the ingested matter, shuttling food in continuous belts below decks for refueling purposes. He hears soft guttural tones and flatulent hues, but he cannot pinpoint their exact whereabouts.

He gets up and walks towards the centipede and gets on his belly and is eye level with his friend and winks at him and examines him and notices the wiggling of certain limbs, and he wonders if the limbs are injured, and he wonders if there's anything he can do, and he wonders why he wants to help, and he falls into a lull, and he falls asleep, and the centipede—inches away from his face—eats and wiggles and carries on undisturbed.

The dream.

He said that there are a lot of midgets around here today, and then he clucked his tongue and rolled his neck from side to side.

She told me he was the best she'd ever had. His penis was long and sharp and praised the wayside routes of her vagina. He said she was the best he'd ever had.

Nowhere does it say I can't run here, that's what the midget told me, and then he ran into a tiny house that looked like an outhouse, but it wasn't an outhouse even though it looked like one.

She looked out a small window from a big stucco house surrounded by big stucco homes on a mountainside overlooking a large sea, and they called it a suburb, and it had a big rock protruding from its guts, and it had a snaking road going up and down its coast, and it was too big to be real, and it dwarfed her and compressed her, and every time a car drove by, it made her sick with vertigo.

Upon waking, the man notices his friend's departure. A murmur of scuttlebutt announces the prologue of an idea, and an incomplete picture forms; potential escape routes jostle for airtime in a fragile imagination with competing parties out to annihilate the others' odds. "Suppose he ate his fill and moved on," deduces the noodle in his noggin at last. He gets up and goes to the refrigerator and puts his paws on an apple and takes a big bite and, with sharp pangs, realizes that the apple is sour as hell.

Question: Was Jesus consummated through the auditory canals of Mary Magdalene as some have speculated?

Chapter 8: The Gods

She was still drunk on youth, dumbing her down to the level of an infantile baboon. And he loved her so much he wanted nothing to do with her.

20 years later... she had attained divinity, a pristine ivory emblem embalmed in a glorious tomb. Transcending the ranks of decomposition, her skeletal remains shone and ennobled her beyond the trivialities of the walking corpses she so despised. They *too* carried with them the same hatred but amassed towards a common goal, rallying towards one technicality or another, never able to unsheathe the final ounce of flesh stuck to the clever bone. Her hatred was pure, unwavering, for it had no destination; it imparted itself inward, cleansing, dispatching the rot, a chastity of pain, hard-won and beautiful—a sainthood reserved for the sad and the wretched.

He was only capable of living by a single principle at any given time, and through years of diligent work, he'd narrowed and perfected the proverb. He summarized it as such: "Each day he must fuck."

No one knew what this meant, although it could've been taken at face value, but he didn't seem like the nympho type. It was even possible, if not probable, that he didn't get laid all that much—at least not by his wife, who seemed to really fucking hate his guts—but maybe "fuck," in this instance, didn't mean the act of fucking and had nothing to do with sex or lovemaking, but actually meant fight or struggle or some other form of the transmuted creative urge, but no one could really tell, and mostly because no one really cared.

And the crowd came at him with intentions of eating his scrawny carcass—bearing meat cleaver and cake fork—they corner him, salivating dribble, and prepare to feast upon the poor sod. Back against the wall, he replies with a tremor, "I'm the hyena of dysentery; chew the cud at your own risk. I'll bend and smite your insides; lay siege to your juvenile guts. Meager fools run afoul; one tiny bite will do you in. I'm a needle point with deadly venom; you're an army rotting from within."

***

He sat next to his two kids and opened the book. He read aloud:

The Story of the Cactus

'Tis an olden tale of a young practitioner's luck,
A benevolent curse hailed from the skies above,
A torrential upheaval of valuable roots,
A conductor's mischievous delirium on display as a ruse.
A signature score derived from the entrails of dismay,
A sacrificial gesture to solidify a name.
A failed plot to receive an echo from above,
A short burst before the final crack, and then the lights go off.

Praise not the story but the structure, or the genesis, or the beautiful, grotesque dance of... and fear not, for those who practice economy practice perfection.

And they loved each other so goddamn much, and they missed each other's smell the most, and then they copulated like rutting elk at high noon.

(At Zenith)

And semen stains the mountaintops or, as some say, God cometh.

And from God's perspective, humanity was a tribe of latent lunatics suffering from a variety of retardations; each and every one of them cast from the shadows of sin and dressed in the hubris of goofy, cacophonous roles, and they came to the same metaphors but spoke with different intonations. And the geometry of their lives, from birth to death, was seen as a solid scripture, carved in postulated hieroglyphs whose esoteric languages spoke from the filaments of the night sky to the unadorned labyrinth of a butt-filled ash-tray. And as God intuited the grand design of existence, from minutiae to millennia, He withdrew into its essence, as the writer withdrew into his fiction, and the dead man into rogue and ghoulish dreams.

And in reference to His creation, the Lord mused on the words of Baudelaire, "An oasis of horror in a desert of boredom." A gift to withdraw into and a target to focus upon.

And in God's wisdom (or boredom or curiosity or an admixture of motives beyond comprehension), God decided to tweak the will of certain chosen folk. As an omniscient entity unbound by time, God relished in the infinitude of cosmic play and fastened complex games of counter logic to the certainties and laws concocted by those dwelling within the Lord's realms. The tale that follows is of such an occurrence; an utterance from God brandishing the coming of a strange and powerful will to a misguided and lost soul.

Chapter 9: The Dwarf Clown

It was the clown who garnered the most applause. He was a dwarf, a calculated force of visual acuity. He was the representation of the claustrophobic Hydra whose heads bore suggestions of prophylactic perjury, daring their decapitation, the copulating violence of slick steel slicing the larynx, a fertile incision, spawning two wherefrom only one once grew.

Note: The description above pertains solely to the karmic deity residing in the soul of our hero, a pregnant platitude bearing no resemblance to his actual physicality. He bears all the normal dwarfish anatomical insignia, a singular rudimentary head fastened to a plump and hearty mortal neck, thereby making him a rather banal-looking archetype. Now onward with the narrative!

The dwarf clown, who shall remain nameless, spoke 6 different languages. As acrobatic nymphs plunged and twirled in the upper regions of the circus tent, the dwarf clown stood some 60 feet below, megaphone in hand, churning out an incomprehensible digression of sounds in a language foreign to the native-speaking audience, frightening their expectations with unapologetic composure and unyielding glee.

The foreign-toothed—or tongued—stranger (the dwarf clown) would inevitably arouse anger and panic amongst the gathered crowd, prompting some worthy patriotic attendee to yell, "Who does this little sombitch think he is? We speak Ein-glash 'round here, bucko!" Cheers and jeers, a camaraderie forms, the brave dialectician, the one who rose from their ranks to speak on their behalf and squash the babble of the idiot dwarf whose nonsense reflected a deep and subversive attitude threatening to bamboozle their illustrious carnivalesque expectations.

The dwarf clown smirks; the crowd is impaired by the frivolity of their discontent, making them a slave to the cause; a hive mind develops and is procured from the buzz of communal anger, seeping from seat to seat, and the dwarf clown stands tall, calmly watching the proceedings develop with haste.

As angry attendees approach ringside, the dwarf clown unsheathes a silver sword, whistling sweet Dixie as he swishes and swashes his swashbuckler's jab, megaphone dropped by the wayside. He beckons them with a revolting smile that insinuates a tremor of madness. They halt, the ringside ringleader (the jeering crowd-pleaser) front and center; his eyes sing with reproachful fear...

Do angels have assholes?
And big, chunky souls?
And sunken blue eyes?
And a pumpernickel nose?

**

He sits alone, bare ass upon the porcelain bowl, sphincter in perpetual thrust, and he whistles a tune, enjoying the biological ride of the moment. He murmurs accompanying words to the melody. The attentive listener able to discern but a few—words like nose or rose, blues and holes. He repeats the verse over and over, and with each new retelling, a change overtakes him. His eyes well up, and his throat is choked, and tears begin to stream down his cheeks. He can't help it; the spell is cast, and its voodoo conducts the accursed dance of the tear ducts in never-ending flow. He buries his face into his hands and (for what feels like an eternity) weeps.

He remains fixed in an emotional purge until an unintended gust of wind breaks from the seam of his asshole. The sound is hostile to the scene at hand and shatters its melancholic structure, leaving him stunned and sober. He looks up and feels silly and strange, and the paradox of moods unzips a profound insight coinciding with the inhalation of the brazen odor escaping from the bowels of the bowl below. He laughs, and as he inhales the fumes, he submits his psyche to strange terrain with maniacal proliferations, usurping with ease past benchmarks of vulgar hilarity as the volume grows and yet another fart reverberates off the porcelain chamber beneath his symphonic sphincter.

***

He had lobotomized his conscious esprit with minute assaults scattered across a decade of drug abuse. Their varied masks assumed the wrappings of pills and book covers, flesh and words. It was a long, slow battle that misrepresented its scale, appearing small but brandishing the iconic double-edged sword of dismay and grief, the swift decapitator of the foulest of foes.

The scales of positivity are most sharply seen under the guise of negativity. Thus spoke the dwarf clown who subsequently brandished his noble blade upon his own person and, with a swift slice, lopped off his left arm.

The fucking blood gushed.

The wound accelerates its flow and sprays endless supplies; the crowd watches, halted, feet wet, rooted in uncertain fates; parents eye wary children, neither moves, blood rises, dwarf clown squirms, blood up past their eyes, a crimson tide, undivided, the dwarf clown dies; an abrupt snap, a resounding crack, an eye-opener and a fresh sight—a loony circumvention back to promised understandings, asses back in seats, original standings—a mental trip, an illusion, a mad magician standing tall. A dwarf clown, with a megaphone, and two arms sewn in proper sockets, with drills for eyes and a serpent for a tongue, a real daemon fiend born Faustian best friend, a coy wink above a cheerful grin, a crowning head peeking back through the veils of a once-bargained-for reality, an extravaganza par excellence catapulted through the doorways of perception—and back again.

They say nothing and blink back enthusiastically and carry awe through dilated pupils, a young boy turns to his mother with questioning eyes, and she responds, saying, "It was just a trick," but he remembers her saying, "Good shit."

Chapter 10: Code Unknown #1

The entities described before are cosmic re-creations of nightmarish beings fashioned in the skull of an oddball television executive whose expertise was Saturday-morning programming. These hideous creatures are unfit for names and require cursory shrugs as a means of dismissive action against the horrors they represent. They have borne themselves deep in the psyche of a generation of youth who don't even know that they're there. They were hatched during hours of uninterrupted television viewings, and his sickness is now your sickness. Talk about a raw deal.

A network of trash becomes the currency for a generation of cellphone hillbillies, yuppie ghetto kings, and pornographic billionaires.

The gods were often bored with their works and hated the works of the others.

One should aspire to at least one act of destruction daily if one is to be considered the creative type.

The proper drug at the proper time, rarely is life ever so kind.

John's life had amassed a wide variety of trivial pursuits, all of which centered on the deplorable need for *more*.

Staring at the mirror and realizing that the composition before your eyes is the exact replica of how the others see you, except for those with vision problems, irrational kinks, strange goals, and superfluous, madness-inducing desires.

THE ROAD TO HELL IS NEVER PAVED.

Chuck the big bug fucks another bug who shits out some more bugs similar to Chuck.

Winter 1994, three boys find the body of a recently deceased neighbor. They poke it with a stick, uncertain and curious, horror escalates from the onset of the incident. Memory transforms and extends the episode; it becomes a metaphor and vehicle for insurmountable dread and unforeseeable violence manifesting in the unconscious of the unlucky three. A note from the dead man's pocket falls out and reads, "I'm so tired."

A good writer contains a multitude of saints, killers, orphans, and hucksters—all in the spherical labyrinth of their bungled-up mind.

"*Do you know my poetry?*"

After ingesting a rather sizable variety of contaminants, our hero sees a large shapeshifting being in the hallway of his apartment building with sharp, agreeable horns.

A prerequisite for creativity is a good pair of walking shoes.

During their last session, he said, "The idea of the moral artist is a contradiction of terms."

At midnight, the whole topsy-turvy enterprise will go up in smoke—and a fire shall consume all interior furnishings. *Why? Rebirths? Who knows?*

One night, George dreamt of a language so beautiful and so terrifying that each word corresponded to an exact spatial moment, perfectly cataloging each event without error, solidifying in its arcane symbols the histories of the world in circular motifs, coded maps of exceptional beauty and accuracy; it existed as an uncountable alphabet of complex characters capable of recreating any given moment in time. A perfect language laying bare the patterns and repetitions of the chaotic world.

Eyes of a serpent,
Tongue of a beast,
Spine of a porcupine,
Gums without teeth.

As longtime friends, they were saddened that their time together was coming to an end. It was the way it had to be because it was the way it was. At least that's what the smarter friend told the other one.

Pharmacists for the masses, long-haul truckers of their own mobile minds.

The TV reached out its claws and slapped him, and then it whispered a strange song... *if it happens, it's supposed to*.

In an attempt to define himself, he divided himself further.

The doorway to a uniquely skewed and cockeyed perspective is the best any artist can offer you.

The couch represented the epicenter of her living room, a place of comfort and ease, where relaxation and lust commingled, and dust bunnies and bedbugs slept.

Driving on carefree highways ranks among the purest pleasures of modern man.

An early sensory experience with traumatic implications exported from Jim's psyche and reconfigured in high-tech, hieroglyphic splendor—that's how the television program described itself.

Creation, as imagined by the ancient Aztecs, was pictorially represented as an orange ball rising from the smashed skull of an old and weathered physician (ticitl), or sometimes just as a disemboweled god.

magicians and writers,
poets and fighters,
align and seek,
satisfaction at the peak.

In the post-apocalyptic landscape, the hordes of humans left live harmoniously together; having seen firsthand the travesties and horrors of real annihilation, they seek communal bliss and cooperation in the heavenly wastelands.

A primitive being at the dawn of creation is given a vision by an unknown god. It sees its successor foraging alone with astral representations guiding its actions. All information is immediately lost in the mind of the beast who's incapable of making heads or tails of the delirium.

Sandy crouched low and smiled, remembering a rhyme her mother had once told her: "Eye for an eye. Tooth for a tooth. Eros is mad, and vengeance is aloof."

Dorothy flexes her muscles and taunts her opponents, aware that they don't have the gall or grit to enter the fight. She is without opponent, endlessly ascending to nowhere.

Having crushed and plundered various cities, Saturn sets out in search of a more majestic metropolis to destroy, scythe and sickle in hand.

In the afterlife, two enemies reconnect in Hades' food court, knowing full well that one of them had killed the other but forgetting which of them was the murderer and which the victim; they decide to bury the hatchet and celebrate the annihilation of their worldly memories with a toast to the loss of their pasts and in praise of their corrupt and degenerate future mindsets.

"The material has a will of its own," said the asshole, and he encouraged it to find its full and unimpeded expression.

A man in olden times is attuned to the Great Weather Forecast. He sits in his ice hut and contemplates the signs in the arctic air and converses with the gods and relishes in their brutal and intoxicating game. He ponders his next move and rubs his whiskered chin, thinking hard about how to outsmart the gods (those ole sons o' bitches) who've become his cunning adversaries and beloved companions.

And he said, "I am on the steps of madness—or deep in a maze-like structure nicknamed the abattoir of forking paths." And he said this to no one in particular, staring up at a grand chandelier with a glazed look in his eye, at a banquet for a retiring coworker he barely knew.

Some have likened life to a game, but what sort of game? And what sort of attributes are most vital, and what's the currency of the scoreboard?

The doctor orders him *not* to drive under the influence of any narcotics, and the coke-sniffing heroin fiend disobeys with ecstatic urgency only to wind up disappointed at having lost his keys.

Memories of a flanking assault. Codename: Bullets Over Mai Tais. A calamity. A trainwreck. Its disastrous execution had led to many deaths in Tom's platoon. He couldn't forget that fateful day nor properly map out the guilty party. Was it his commanding officer whose plan was ill devised? Or was it simply bad luck and a poor twist of fate? Was it God's doing? All three questions couldn't provide a soothing answer, nor a proper scapegoat, as the memories of that day had cut right through the better part of Tom's already dwindling supplies of hope and benevolence and shattered much of his former psyche, which he'd cobbled together again—as best he could—with duct tape and wire. How could one repair what was irrevocably damaged? Tom thought of how treacherous life was when a single 24-hour period could lay waste to the accumulated stores of one's humanity.

An angel known as Jacinta eyes the world with concern and sadness but feels little ambition to intercede.

Jerry sits on his grandmother's stoop and imagines the genesis of a supervillain.

It existed more like an unreal dream than a concrete memory, twisted and romanticized with the years.

Improve it—or shut the fuck up.

The ass looks away as the masters disembowel one another.

Time as a forced perspective.

And it enters the soft tissue of the brain...

And this is the story of many Georges.

George's brain was rarely given enough sleep and during waking hours it often lolled along, floating above the events surrounding it. Often only registering the goings-on minutes or even hours later with latent and restrictive responses that made his coworkers and friends look at him as if he were a certified idiot.

Twins who've aged along the same compulsory trajectory for 30-plus years decide to intervene in God's plan. Their scheme involves forcing a divide—making Twin A ingest an *inhuman* amount of toxic and mind-altering substances, all the while letting his hair grow any which way it wishes. They sense that this will force a detour in God's plan and irrevocably change their wills.

Change your hair, change your life.

The television offered a direct stream into the collective psyche in its most mundane and honest form.

Fire, fire burning bright,
Save us from encroaching night.

Even at 35, Olivia understood why some people might kill themselves and that all groups, in one form or another, contained many assholes.

Lonely Louis' best pal was an outlaw cockroach named Charlie who scurried along his apartment floors at all hours of the night and seemed to have an unusually long lifespan, or maybe he just confused Charlie with other cockroaches, as there wasn't much to distinguish one from another.

A bull in his dream asks him a strange question. Something like, "*How come you didn't fuck her, pansy*?" He has no idea who the bull is referring to but feels insulted and ashamed nonetheless. He tries to respond, but the bull will have none of it, and suddenly the scene dissolves, and he's standing on an empty country road in the dead of night, or maybe he's in a pitch-black Byzantine ballroom; he can't really tell.

The first sign of vegetation from a supposedly barren landscape is an ugly and desaturated flower.

She smiles coquettishly, hiding her head and trying hard to divert the expressions flashing across her face. He will see the truth, she thinks, and she tries hard to cry or laugh or fart or anything that will dissuade him from seeing the reality of her feelings. She is a faltering master of dissimulation.

God surfs the pipeline of a utopian porcelain bowl.
—graffiti at the base of a dirty public toilet

Inanimate objects speak in Russian slang so as not to be overheard by the rodents and vermin scuttling around the kitchen.

"Это фикция опечаток. Победитель, победитель, куриный ужин."

Perceptions, or varying degrees of madness.

Rivers and telephones worked along the same lines and whispered hidden phrases like, "Don't be afraid of happiness, it doesn't exist," and other such half-truths.

Bewilderment and disappointment were often slapped across the poor schmuck's face. And his idiotic appraisal of life, along with his positive attitude, routinely meant that life held the upper hand—smashing the poor bastard whose stupidity both assured his destruction and allowed for a hopeful, if not misguided, resurrection after each embarrassing defeat.

Personality trumps rhetoric.

Mankind was fettered by a frenzied need to persist.

And they were all desperate people but desperate in all the wrong ways.

***

The twins' plan did not go as planned, and as an act of defiance against their Creator, they each took their life, ending their suffering... or so they thought. Little did they know, God had other ideas and trapped them in a hell specifically tailored to their hubris; He gave them each an astonishing gift (clairvoyance, rejuvenation, etc.) while imbuing it with the seed of their destruction in some ironic or horrible manner. Think the daily torment of Prometheus with the eagle eating his regenerating liver, over and over again, and you get the idea. God was not always original, although He was generally quite effective.

They made love under the stars and under the cobwebs of the cosmos, and they grinned at one another, grateful for their luck and repose.

Unknown to the moose, it was currently playing host to a vile brain-eating parasite worming its way through its head.

An unknown friend tells George that in order to improve his life, he'll have to make some changes, starting with his diet, exercise regimen, friends, financial status, social activities, demeanor, fashion, gait, and dick size.

Young Timmy gives a soothsaying machine a quarter and waits patiently as the animatronic doll gives him less than satisfactory advice from immobile lips.

Blissful bike rides through empty mall parking lots were integral to Tom's adolescent development.

The apple was not as the snake had described it.

Angels circled streetlamps like moths to a flame, and one was hard-pressed to call these winged creatures divine based on their chaotic and unnerving flight patterns.

John, Judy, Joan, Jack, Joyce, Jim, Julie, and Louie.

Dr. Hilarius points to the Snellen chart, and Gwen has

great difficulty reading and regurgitating the fourth row downward.

The vermin remain deaf to the world of mass-produced kitchenware.

Escape the menagerie,
Machete in my hand,
Beware the schism,
I'm the Jungle Man.
—note found in tenant's refrigerator

His first night in town, he stayed at an elegant hotel not far from the docks and drank copiously at the hotel bar. He talked to a young lady whose strategy for a good life consisted mainly of knowing when and how to put on the right face for the right instant. She told him that she had over a thousand masks at her disposal at any given moment.

Afterwards—tired and a little drunk—he went up to his room, jerked off, and then looked through the sports channels on an old television set.

And God descended and He cleansed the lands and the pigs looked up in envy.

Jacinta, the angel, still sits waiting, contemplating each and every one of her options, realizing that if she does act and acts wrongly, she could cause more harm than good, but if she withholds action and her intervention is necessary, she would nonetheless be guilty of committing an act of evil. The whole thing was a bit silly and narcissistic; could one angel really make a difference? Maybe, but then again, on a long enough timeline, all actions, like the muddled noise from a boisterous crowd, lose their meaning, and any orientation towards good and evil are thus simply stepping-stones, propelling events onto events, good producing evil, and vice versa, in a long and seemingly endless chain.

Activists take to the streets in hopes of communicating their point through disruption, volume, and sheer noise.

A mask becomes the face and conceals nothing beneath it.

For Claude, the apex of art was erotic and sterile. A cold vacuum of animalistic impulses seen with a surgeon's eye.

Walking through the city helped Joan understand the territory and separate it from the symbols and geometry of the map. Territories held many interesting revelations that no man-made or computer-based map could yet aspire to overtake, most notably smells and the possibility of strange (mostly innocuous) encounters—in other words, the physical aspects of actually maneuvering your body through space. Perhaps, in the future, maps would evolve and somehow implement this sensory component. Then she thought of how this had already begun, how videogames interpreted both, although to a lesser degree, with piloted characters physically going through their virtual worlds (rumbling controllers and surround sound) pushing towards checkpoints or goals or simply guided by some wayward idea of progress or exploration—a simulacrum or a version of a version of a life. Yet who knew what future marvels or nightmares could be unearthed in these technological worlds; as the old ancestral ways separated themselves further and further from modern man's reality, was there even a point in getting upset? Was this progress? Was it a good thing? At its core, would it actually make that big of a difference for her? Joan wasn't sure, although she sensed that she would continue in her old ways regardless, as computers and screens held little interest for her.

Lying alone in his apartment with soothing visions induced by too much TV.

She always felt that her talents would lend her an opportunity to distinguish herself from her peers—and, to some degree, they did, although she still felt suffocated in this game whose goal of reaching some imaginary height was often depressing and handicapping.

Bert the Bee buzzes around in hopes of finding the right flower to pollinate; bored and a little tired, he knows he will probably stop soon, but before he does, he will be hit by a semi-truck and splatter against its windshield.

An army of Sisyphus-like creatures attempts the arduous task of rolling a boulder, yet again, up the mountain. Because God has calmed down in His old age, He gives them a break and allows them each a finite amount of prescription pills to stimulate a sense of euphoria and energy. The pills rejuvenate in a magic pillbox He has bestowed to each of the creatures only when the boulder has rolled back to its initial starting position. What was once the symbol of a hopeless and trifling task now represents the drug fiend's joy at having scored another hit.

The All-Powerful Being rises from the depths and reaches out its cartoon hand, ready to bestow good familiars to its conjurors and smite any fools careless and stupid enough to get in the way of its ascension.

"Awake, dear friend, and seize the goddamn day!"

Chapter 11: Some Questions Will Kill You Outright

He would rather the tender whore than the loyal wench, and so Joe, exterminator extraordinaire, sought the company of young Judy Dwyer, daughter of Mortimer and Sabbath Dwyer and heiress to a fortune of disenfranchised ideals governing the lion's share of the young mademoiselle's strange topographic fate. She embraced Joe with open arms each morning but was rarely seen when he resurfaced from work later in the day. Instead, she entered the bedroom at odd hours of the night; smells of an alarming sort accompanied her as she made haste to snuggle alongside the contours of her darling Joe, who accepted her with a snore and a quick reshuffle, as she entered the darkness of her dreams with a whistling exhale and a cockeyed grin.

Their dreams tended towards the jazzy and arcane sort, or those of a rapscallion's nightmare.

They lived on pod colony 1216. A stilted monolithic empire housing a growing populace 40 or so feet above the earth's surface with giant slabs of rock fostering the foundation for these wayward people's civilized lives.

And the architect was an aging ectomorph who'd built the hub for the survivors of the last great fallout on the edge of the boreal forest and was said to be both an ascetic and a madman. He lived in the topmost corner facing the roaring waves and was rumored to only appear among the populace under the guise of various prosthetic noses.

"Morals, like anything rigid, could sink the ship too."

Teenagers spray-painted a plethora of slogans and aphorisms around the colony's walls and ridges.

She was fascinated by the promiscuity of words. The way they tended and tied.

"Because I can, I did.
If you could, you would."
—assertion of will

He rode the Route 66.
(Erode the root, itssickitssick)
—written on a bathroom stall

She took a sniff of cocaine to the rear of her septum,
straight from the source,
in a bar named Rectum.

It was the only bar on pod colony 1216. It had two broken sinks and housed a down-on-their-luck band of rogue canines, a conglomerate of lost terriers squatting together between dumpster dives and all-out back-alley orgies.

She was lulled by his beauty and lured by his body, but she lusted for the dullness of his misshapen eyes.

And they found her cascading on the carcass of a deformed tree trunk with arrowheads piercing her body, and the words "Conquerors of the East" scraped across a darkened 2x4 at the base of this contorted monument.

And young Judy Dwyer was pronounced dead at the scene; puncture wounds and lacerations notwithstanding, her eyes, alert and hollow, bore no signs of lingering distress. She had persisted for 26 years under the constant murmur of an unerring heartbeat until her line had led her to this abandoned altar only a few yards from pod colony 1216's entranceway, and her darling Joe—now grieving exterminator and whimpering sod—had begotten a desire in his depths; under the spell of the murderer's violent tableau, a gestating North Star now beat heartily and aligned his arc towards a dim future full of grisly and excessive bloodshed.

And he thought, "You sometimes have to sacrifice the best parts of yourself, and it's rather horrible," and then he thought, "A wish to do good could be the root of an unseemly anger," and finally, "I now have a blind purpose to match my iron will."

Detective 12: Murderers? You suspect more than one perpetrator?
Detective 8: But of course, look at the lewdness of the scene and the grandeur of its style. I suspect a whole court of jesters.

***

Jester #1: We Are All Self-Destructive Animals
Stripped of his title, he was afraid of his own fur. Philip, a dismal chap, unwavering in his subservience to those of the

most powerful and disagreeable rank, a political weasel and a pompous braggart; he was easily herded and had a strength for assimilation—he possessed little in the realm of enviable scruples beyond a meek and meandering sense of survival. A tip from a reliable source placed Philip firmly at the scene.

He had watched on, cheering as the others had laid siege to young Judy Dwyer's corporeal being. Before Joe thrust his axe deep into the trunk of poor slobbering Philip, he let it be known that four other miscreants were involved: Vincent, Theo, Paul, and Michael.

Jester #2: The Doctors Are Dead and the Lunatics Control the Asylum

There's no certainty, that's for certain, but probability could save the day, and Joe found Vincent well cocooned on the pot, as predicted, unloading digested bits of Taco Tuesday; a ritual he suffered from on a weekly basis because of his poorly chosen, albeit cheaply acquired, fast-food diet.

Jester #3: 1-800-Hello-Architects

Theo begged Jim for his life and admitted a defective nature and a malleable sense of right and wrong as the true culprits. He let slip that various spectators and neighbors had all stood 'round watching young Judy Dwyer's demise. If he were to be held accountable, surely they should be too. Jim was tired of listening to such babble and chopped him up into little, itty-bitty bits and spread him out around Rectum for the lost dogs to lap up as nutritious, protein-rich chow.

Jester #4: Magixbug

His tongue was tied, but his eyes told the truth, and Jim could see Michael's stoic nature and resigned disposition shine through and accept his terrible fate. This did little to appease Jim's scorn, and his axe fell hard, just as it had for the others and would presumably continue to for so many more.

Jester #5: There's No Devil in Outer Space

He decided to start fresh and blow up the dams and brew a seething fire in the heart of the woods surrounding pod colony 1216.

The habitat—along with its inhabitants—was being eaten by the elements, and its destruction marked its creator's ascension beyond mere prideful and caustic rage to a realm of mythic and violent quietude, a transition from one reign to the next.

A tyrant towards guilt, he eviscerated its scrotum with the crux of his monstrous blade, and he closed its mouth forever.

Jester #6: And thou shall know thy true God, and thou shall be devoured in true horrorshow fashion, when terror becomes tedium, and the ballet reaches her sublime and dismal peak, a decadent satanic verse (or the marriage of heaven and hell).

He was an exacting poet, existing somewhere between Archimedean priest and hunchbacked sailor. A surveyor of strange fevers, his soul bore a conspiratorial spiral, unraveling in circular misadventures, distancing him evermore from the common shore with each tick of the monotonous clock.

It was said that his artistry existed outside the confines of most circumstantial time zones. It bore him back to the original misstep, the fallen icon, or the noble rot. Man's true drive, born of instinct, not intellect. Adam's prized offspring watching the waves crash and the fires burn with a satiated sense of a mislabeled paradise finally being brought to justice and down to the barrenness of its wonky knees. In accordance with canonical rites, stripped of its pomp and swagger, it swayed under the shadow of its former self, heralding its newfound executioner, the heavy-metal exterminator, who loaded the weight of his axe with a calculated backswing and a huge, exaggerated inhale.

And in his final moments of lucidity, he understood the origin of his strength, the arteries fashioned in the deep and harnessed in the pulpit of mud and humiliation.

And words from an ancient philosopher were called forth to his mind, "*If a tiger could speak, we could not understand it.*" And just then, his nose fell off.

Chapter 12: Hell
(or the Violent Bear It Away)

Should her spirit not have earned a better final fate?
Had she not been a keen and passionate young fool?
Or are rewards only for the just and wise soul?
And not the blunted and disenfranchised tool?

The sight is incredible and augmented by its form possessing no discernable center; as landscapes fall willy-nilly along rotating paths, all unglues from cohesion. Islands fall, float, and spin, while others remain stationary only to succumb to the same rotary fate when properly focused upon. Disorientation develops into normalcy, and the goggles of hell fall upon their victim.

Joan's brain wanders in a multitude of directions and remains unfixed as existential questions and indecipherable links to terrestrial memories doom her motion-sick mind to a plethora of vague and inconsequential anomalies. She falls to her knees and notes the soil beneath her for the first time as a worm, as large as a snake, pokes through and mirrors her swaying motion with its eyeless head. It opens its beak and lets out a drowned honk, which inexplicably comforts her.

It was an odd marriage; a deranged Sisyphean drug-dream of worm and woman coaxed together, warped into union as a fashionable faux pas on a creature feature from Plan 9. The others, or those of the sentient persuasion residing upon the selfsame floating rock, did not wear worms as scarfs, but neither did they seem to judge Joan's choice of companion, as each individual, with the noted exception of Joan herself, seemed to be confined to their own individual delirium, noticing little or none of their surrounding circumstances.

"You can't trust morality 'round here," spoke the worm in its own indubitable manner. It did not necessitate the use of any known language but had, over the years, developed a partnership of systemic pulsings in which the tensing of its muscles, along with the punctuated notes of its flat mucus-based drones, had grown into a complex tongue overriding Joan's intuitive ways. Her thoughts had become less and less pictographic, reverting to more primitive and sensuous means of assemblage.

***

Joyce and company developed under the curious conditions of hell, and their former attributes waned. A mote of red celestial debris, tentatively called Jupiter, passed in a continuous loop overhead and exacted the means by which their time was measured and tried.

The inhabitants had a habit of changing the names of the objects existing within their plane. Shifting sounds and symbols designated shifts in tonal degrees, and the altering effect was good at staving off boredom for the eternal occupant.

Joyce and her star pupil were merging more and more with each completed loop of the Zeus Star, and the reign of the worm was close at hand.

A once-preliminary accessory,
Yielded beyond the complementary,
And drove as the primary mold,
Melting the pie.
A blindworm fused upon the pure,
Damned its host,
And stole her right eye.

Dost thou seek a hindrance for thy soul, an antidote for thy repose?

Would ye like a more rambunctious trek, a soliloquy, or perhaps its antipode?

The worm was now in complete control and dictated the ends by which Joan, or Joyce, or Judy, or whoever's former corporeal reality it had sought, was to be displayed. It had hijacked an orphan being and courted it until its matrimonial obligations had distilled and discarded its tenant's former history. Vacancy in a place such as this was in limited supply.

In the *tête-de-Joan*, a dejected thought echoed about in a disgraceful dance.

"Everyone wants to rape the angels. What the hell's going on here?"

"An epidemic of earnest charlatans and pseudo-pranksters have taken the wheel," said the worm.

Time to meet your God.

She wore new eyes that bore her forward along some inevitable timeline. A drunken doll dancing with déjà vu, a prime puppet for our parasite par excellence—a malicious painter turned punisher held an apocalyptic hymn so near a point as the tip of her tongue. A rogue feeling and a vengeful urge unfurled her riddle, gave it birth, and at last, the requiem was sung.

The gigantic rocks began to coalesce towards Jane. The worm's song had untethered the natural orbit, and a mandala of destruction rerouted all mass towards her; the center would not hold forever, but the imminent path of astrological doom held Jane captive as the incumbent orator of the current order.

The sky was pitch-black and seething with distress. Other inhabitants were acquitted from their former shackles, and the larks glimpsed their fate. Shouts and groans were displaced by the natural immensity of giants coming together.

Some illusions are better left undisturbed... at least for now.

She woke up alone, ignorant of the denouement that had befallen her. A persona non grata to that particular stem of the lobe. A gladiator whose historic battle lay meek and withered—a barren coward under the cosmos—its existence a mere conjecture whose former witnesses lay buried beneath, slain relics, as Jane, an amnesiac with embellished parlance, relished in the doom of their defeat.

She was a whore to tone.

A goddess, a destroyer.

Hail, the Queen! (or the Thin Pink Duke!)

Chapter 13: The Detective & the Killer

Most loons aren't that strong, but he was strong for a loon, particularly in the domain of mental fortitude. And he knew when to yield and when to make haste and when to depart and when to chop 'em down. A brute of a boy, a champ of a lad, a real up-and-comer.

And he said, "Anyone who wasn't going to rise with it would fall by it."

There are no good or bad people, just bad directions.

And there are no good or bad lions, just bad days.

And he wasn't an agent of chaos so much as a weirdly wired and misdirected soul with a strange limp and kooky, deep-set eyes, sent forth to dictate the scrambled order of the day with an iron fist and a large bowie knife.

***

He is 36 and has a strong proclivity for violence. He dreams of nymphets and angels and rabid dogs with invisible tails and keeps an assortment of sharpened tools within arm's reach of his boudoir. His name is Gord, but in his mind, he calls himself Ellen. He had a strange dream the night before about two baby brothers. One of whom begins to crush the other, who in turn becomes as flat as a pancake and takes on the consistency of microwaved pizza. The pummeling brother then devours the deep-dish remains of his kin without the least bit of hesitation or remorse.

Gord woke up from the dream burping and nauseous.

A recent conversation with Gord.

Gord: Everyone needs a nemesis and who better than the mutinous militiamen with amnesiac tendencies squatting in the crux of my meandering noggin.

"Exactly," mutters Ellen. "Exactly."

And he looked at her and knew her head held the hoax of an intellect, but that didn't seem to bother him any, if at all.

**

She had the brain of a psychopath but the body of a saint.

And her brain told her that it was important not to look the part. And that a good trip held many horrors, like a hall of mirrors or a haunted house at a cheap traveling carnival; and that this was the epitome of bliss for someone like her—a dick, a PI, a state-sanctioned detective, or a local cop working the beat—someone with their own brand of justice and neurosis, and that that was okay, better than okay, and she told herself that her talents were valuable although somewhat undesirable, and they would often be disapproved of or, at the very least, misunderstood.

And when she thought of cleanliness being next to god-liness, she thought of the foolishness of the statement and the foolishness of folk who spit out such nonsense, and she kept a small heap of dust in the corner nook of her apartment as a reminder of the ensuing disorder sur-rounding her ordinary, routinized world. God was chaos or, at the very least, incomprehensible and therefore a hazard of misunderstandings and colluded ideologies corrupted, misassembled, and fused together by confusion, anger, and good or mock intentions. The dust took on a shrine-like essence, like sanctified ash, and in peak daylight hours—when the sun shined directly onto it—it could make her go gaga, or gag with maniacal laughter, or masturbate surreptitiously without pause.

Her power of detection came from a discerning sense of selective apathy and a resilient strain of nomadic hope.

And her brain told her that there are no stupid thoughts, just insane ones.

It's Monday, and she wakes up and scrubs her skin and drives to the Oksana Barge Sheriff's Station. She is a deputy sheriff, and she's hot on the trail of the local psy-chopath, a knife-wielding maniac known throughout the region as Jim. She suspects Jim to be an unassuming lad, a regular bimbo Joe, donning the part of local hell-raiser, the debutante of mischief and mayhem, and for some godforsaken reason, this morning at least, she feels a kinship towards him, but she shakes off this lunacy with a couple of stray cigarettes and a few big swigs of cold, acidic coffee. He's a right crackerjack psycho, she thinks, and she wonders what's this connection flickering in her gut, and she hopes to find an innocuous answer to this disturbing and sentimental puzzle.

She takes a left on Richmond Lane and rolls down the window and takes in 5 or 6 good deep breaths, and she eyes the surrounding mountains and continues down a dirt road in slow and bumpy fashion, snagging rogue branches among the multitude of pines, sipping fresh coffee in a tin cup from a doughnut shop called El Nuevo, heading alone to God-knows-where, in a rusty truck, through a treacherous and thick fucking forest.

***

He wanted to be the first kid on his block to get a confirmed kill.

And he knew that a well-placed sentence, or a well-placed word, or even a playfully shot bullet, could irrevocably change the world. It was this sort of sentiment that earned him praise among the higher-ups of the Marine Corps.

And his God was the God of order, a perfect God, a God of cause and effect originating from a single purpose rippling out through the cosmos and guiding destiny with an assured and focused hand. Freedom was a dream wasted on the weak, and he, a Marine, knew better than to harbor such gross and uncanny ignorance. During his training, he excelled, although he was first deemed a pigeon-toed faggot, or Private Fluffy, by his superior officers, but later, after weeks of humping his way through basic training, he was said to have become a terrifying specimen, a merchant of death if ever there was one. He graduated and was sent overseas to kill Charlie, and during his flight, he dreamt of a girl from his block whose pubis smelt of distinct and forbidden musk.

He knew he would have to lose his mind or his balls, and he chose his mind, or his mind chose for him, and he became an albatross in the jungles haunted by the Viet Cong, soaring ever higher with each dead gook, killing for honor and freedom and everything in between. And he, along with his fellow countrymen—White, Black, Hispanic—united, fighting for the cause, enraptured by the sanctimonious game of deadly combat. A puritanical activity if ever there was one. He didn't love it, but he had been shaped by it, adapted to it, bit by bit, on foreign soil no less, and he knew that any sudden deviation from this kill-or-be-killed game would be unkind and cruel to his newfound mental apparatus. It had evolved beyond the sheer macabre and now employed a carnivorous black hole governing its depths—unyielding and malevolent—a soul bearing "The Void" (as fashionable parlance would have it), beyond the aid of modern coercive techniques and verbal probes; lusting with insatiable hunger, he hung like a lonely monkey at the founding baobab tree, glowing crimson in patriotic garb and cloaked and reeling in the machinery of war. He smiled an insane smile at his commanding officer who patted him on the back, nodding affirmatively, and said, "Good work, son."

He noticed her in the courtyard. She was very pretty, borderline beautiful.

***

While driving in search of the elusive abode, she thought of a game she used to play in the playgrounds of her youth with an assortment of rude and laudable children, screaming and yelling in what was surely the echoes of childish bliss. They acted out an orienteering game in which one individual, the chosen *it*, would yell directives with their eyes closed. "4 steps forward," he or she would yell. "Jump to your right!" Most kids stuck to the ground while the bravest, vainest, and dumbest mounted the playset, increasing the height of their ascent for higher kicks and peer points among the rebels and children of the grade school. The game's most memorable accolades claimed the virgin bones of a handful of rogue and righteous kids who were forced to jump from the topmost platforms when yells of "Jump backwards!" permeated the playground air. Few victims of the jump became repeat offenders, except for a few souls too callous to call it quits— usually those who in later years would either conquer life's various sectors or succumb to its lowest forms of depravity.

She was that magical mix of fascist hippie and gentle, down-home conservative, and she was wary of any place where everyone was dressed the same. She was constantly improving herself, playing and reshuffling the pieces and molesting her darkest attributes as fodder for self-improvement, and she knew to withhold the entirety of her judgment until she could look the offender square in the eye, slapping on the cuffs, and if they were real baddies, maybe she'd add a couple of extra whacks from her trusty baton.

She parks her truck at the end of the driveway and strolls cautiously up the front steps. She knocks to a 5/8 time signature, and the killer lets her in.

If a tiger eats a zebra,
And a car kills a moose.
And a junkie injects vitamins,
And a madman gets loose.

What's the cause of this chaos?
Is the pattern preordained?
Are morals hubris and sophistry?
Does this jungle have another name?

"And how do you take over the world?" she asked.

"Through violence and patience, mademoiselle. Focused on the bodily and/or spiritual domains."

"But do you really want to be cast as the villain of the story?"

"Necessary roles, my dear, based on the whims of the narrator and the predilections of the mob. Best to contest oneself solely with vocational matters and develop the craft. Where one spends his or her time is the well from which one drinks, so be careful what you get good at."

"To die in music and be absorbed in dreams."

—madman's babble, or beautiful babel

"It was a delicate balance of intricate flavors and subtle harmonies, a striking ebb and flow." And she pulsed his seared organs with cream and cognac in a Walmart blender and smeared the mousse over an organic saltine. She was a salivating cannibal bred in the decadence of the modern era, and we all loved her for it.

Now burn the witch! spoke the bitch with a twitch, whose center was everywhere and circumference unknown.

And she ate him, and he began his journey south through venerated digestive tubes en route to the perfunctory anus. And she thought, "Time has a way with us all," and the detective marked the occasion with a high-angle selfie as the killer assimilated within.

(Burp!)

Chapter 14: Richard the 2nd

The hair on his face cast a long shadow, a dark pedigree of disorder distorting the outgoing calls. He nodded to the teller and picked up his pack of cigarettes.

He'd been trying to kill himself for years and walked around a full-time failure.

He was an odd duck, a misarranged economic nightmare of odds and ends in which power equated to cowardice and virtue to powerlessness.

"What the jumpin' Jehoshaphat?"

Richard learned punishment as a rectifying exercise, righting misaligned switches along the canals of his persona with each incoming blow. A gambling, self-consuming misanthrope, all in for better or worse.

His dick would only get hard around very specific arrangements. He said he had a tricky cunt, and no goddamn pill under the sun would set it like it used to be. But every so often, it'd blossom from its slumber under the right momentary chaos.

He noted that wisdom often camouflaged itself as non-sense, while nonsense cloaked itself under a shiny veneer of horseshit.

He was 82 years old, the old rascal, and they called him Richard, but he had little use for the name now. His goddamn hearing was gone, or so he told anyone who mustered the courage to approach the old coot. "I can't hear a fuckin' thing you're saying," he'd say, imbuing the conversation with such finality that very few wished to continue beyond this point.

His granddaughter gave him goggles to put on and a stick with buttons to hold. She said he'd enter a new plane of existence; a virtual world of demons and loot where murder equated to points and brutality sought the hierarchy of the leaderboard.

After killing numerous pixelated persons, he took off the goggles and noticed that he had a serendipitous erection.

By becoming a smack addict during the late 1970s, he'd relied heavily upon the kindness of a vast array of diverse dealers in order to procure his fix. He noted the laxity in which he and his fellow addicts viewed the racial and gender politics of the time. They had a simple goal and were blind to the hand that fed them.

He lived in what could certainly be deemed a sanitarium, in the heart of a town nicknamed Sodom, on an allowance of sophisticated frugality, through times of systematic senility.

Richard enjoyed walking down the street and imagining tangential lives in which he'd endow the passing pedestrians with prime roles in his peachy saga.

Wives, brothers, fathers, mothers, lovers, daughters, and sons, among others.

Once upon a blue moon, he passed a Hasidic-Jew-cum-transvestite and promptly contemplated himself under such a guise. He concluded that it would be an interesting life and placed it among his preferred reincarnations.

While his granddaughter sat on his lap, he told her, "In times of trouble, remember a sonnet. You may be preacher, but I am prophet."

(Not really a sonnet.)

His mind was tuned to a strange frequency that captivated none but a cursed few, eccentrics and weirdos of their epoch, mineral miners of the zeitgeist's disturbed imagination. Under the pretense of a restful state of mind, they chipped away at the incoming code—manic workers deciphering one elixir after another, bottled and corked for their personal use, half-crazed and incapable of much else, hosts and victims to an unquenchable thirst and sometimes a marketable byproduct.

***

Imaginings:

He sat on an old recliner, upholstered in the fashion of the nuclear glory days when dreams and luxury coexisted as an asphalt lane tending towards success and manageable happiness.

Militant morals were inlaid upon the foundation and secreted in codes, debunking freedom as virtue and orienting it towards vice. Although superficialities were discarded and reconfigured *à la mode du jour*, laxity for perverse thought, however prevalent within the human psyche, was at an all-time low. One could wear whatever one wanted, fuck whom-ever one chose, travel anywhere, occupy most (if not any) positions, and yet, with so much possibility and movement, foresight and wisdom were relegated to the back seat. Shoddy patchwork was dispatched to garish wounds festering with terminal infection.

She came in delirious with a drunken smile, high on a glucose binge as her parents held her upright with morose expressions plastered across their mugs, a broken hymen of panic combusted in each of their irises. Richard stood up from his recliner and donned his surgical scrubs and set about sharpening his tools. He told them to lay her on the table; the wounds on her leg leaked pus and bore the signs of hardened mutilation beyond the bounds of repair.

Diabetes of the spirit. Cut and cauterize.

He picked up the severed limb, independent and permanently altered from the history of that of its host. He looked at the deformed youth who wore an angelic and dreamy expression, yet undisturbed by her sudden metamorphosis, breathing quietly in an inundated state of drug-induced slumber.

It saddened him to administer the amputation and canonize events such as these in the lives of his patients. The lancer of limbs saved lives but at a precarious cost often associated with a great deal of pain.

He wished her all the best and recited a short prayer, a hopeful plea for salvation.

He passed out in the recliner, still donning his blood-soaked garb, and dreamt of Saint Peter while he waited for the next poor soul to burst in.

Chapter 15: Nirvana (in Heaven, Everything Is Fine)

She could alchemize any longing within a distance of three feet and led an exhaustive life. She delighted in the use of her keen, albeit untimely, imagination and mixed rambunctious overtones with her many means and manners. She mitigated and agitated and provoked a renewal of courtships and provocations among the dancing guests gleaming through her sardonic haute-couture world.

***

It didn't make any sense that she should be where she was. Everything was distorted and blue.

Gwen: Where am I?

Her voice rang out and echoed from some unidentifiable point only to return muffled and transfigured, perceptively different from the one she knew as her own.

Gwen: What happened to me?

She continued down her questionnaire in hopes that her bizarre predicament could be explained by someone, anyone, just a few answers to seemingly simple questions.

Nothing recognizably tangible appeared; a curtain of blue enveloped her and bore no measurable dimensions. It felt bafflingly close and impossibly far. It pulsed with obnoxious rhythms.

It was outside the bounds of anything she could have dared imagine; an ocean unstuck from the fabric of the humble, workaday world; offended by the fellowship of the natural order, it wore an expression of chaos and disarray. It disfigured itself in a somber shade, preening itself based on past benchmarks of ancient magic and high culture; a fashionable code of ineffectual ruins tied together with hypnotic pizazz and dressed in an indecipherable cloak of mock futility.

It was offended by her humility and above her petty licentiousness.

***

Results dissipated, some faster than others, but the inevitable decline was sure to ensue at one point or another. Her goal had suffered a serious blow from the clutches of entropy, but through sheer perseverance and perverted will, she sought the reverse route, edging her towards a secret science and a holy order. As long as she was still kicking, she could continue to build her ark and develop her most palatable and enduring sequence. Futility be damned; what the hell else was there to do, anyway?

She was spurring her interlocutor forward, a code unknown, urging them through a strange hoodwinking of neon fairy tales and ghastly stars. She decided to throw an independent and undependable maneuver their way. She shifted the curtain and performed reckless miracles before their eyes and cautiously awaited the verdict.

***

The curtain began to move and shake about in dramatic fashion. It dissolved and revealed a daunting stage. A scene from her youth that she hadn't thought about in decades. Borne beneath and now miraculously appearing before her spellbound eyes. Snowflakes were falling; she was no more than 12; the night sky hung thick, and she sat quietly in an idling station wagon, listening to the radio, awaiting her mother to return from the pizzeria, fetching their Wednesday night supper: one large vegetarian and one medium pepperoni pizza.

The car breaks free from the parking lot and heads west on Highway 49. Gwen sees a billboard that reads, "How many parasites can you withstand?" She takes a heavy whiff of fragrant cheese and greasy salami, at peace in the coupe de ville of her dreams, putt-putting along heavy snowbanks and luminescent street signs.

It's 1993 in a beautiful winter wonderland.

The radio announces the arrival of an insipid song, a nasty ditty *au goût du jour*. Gwen eyes her mother, and they reproach the beat in unison. Gwen pushes a tape into the cassette deck, and life is golden, at least for now, in this pristine pop-infused saga.

They stop at the video store; her mother's instructions underline the quickness in which the selection process must be undertaken; piping-hot pizza is at stake. Gwen nods and understands the severity and accepts the condensed timeframe. She disembarks from the station wagon and glides along icy sidewalks towards Movieland's dense glass entranceway.

They finish watching the gory thriller *Carnal Rage 2: Mechanically Enhanced*; both mother and daughter lie lethargically prone on cotton-clad loveseats. Eyes combat drowsiness, and soft snores develop as the credits roll, and Gwen fades into a strange and frightful dream.

She is in the middle of a snow-drenched highway. An approaching orb veers steadily towards her, and as it approaches, Gwen notices some peculiarities about its make and model. One being that its headlights are not actual headlights and are, in fact, nefarious reptilian eyes.

"It's a goddamn snake dream," says a voice in the dream. "And the goddamn snake is going to eat you, and there's nothing you can do about it. Resign yourself, brave girl! For you are God's Slim Jim. Sack up and be devoured honorably."

When she wakes up on the couch, she is crying, and her mother is still asleep. She is terrified and believes the dream to be a prophetic vision. She wants to wake her mother and tell her about it, but she's certain there is nothing she can do. For the rest of the night, Gwen continues to enter the degrading dream, passing in episodic chunks along the digestive canal of some giant worm-like monster—catastrophically (and claustrophobically) pushed and prodded—she suffocates and disintegrates to an eerie soundtrack straight from the boiler room.

And then everything was heavenly... distorted and blue... and once again the curtains began to shake.

"I dreamt I was a butterfly,
With 8s sewn in my sides,
An intricately woven thread,
I soar above the tide."
—7th grader's journal

It was good to see some familiar folk at the curtain call, thought Gwen.

And the theme?

Digestion.

And outside of the diner, a regal raven croaked.

Chapter 16: The Princess

Outside in the distance, a castle lies decrepit and worn, inhabited by a lost princess whose ancestry is unknown.

She was resigned to a despondent will and kept away from the group, and she bore her curse in quiet solitude in the highest tower of the lowliest rank.

After the meal, she sat satiated near the edge of her cell. She glimpsed the sun from unknown horizons and greeted the freedom of a brief hopeful moment. And she thought, "Everyone needs coping mechanisms even for just a little bit."

Her reign began with an epoch of filth.

A potential suitor came through her window one night, and he told her of many curious things. In particular, she remembered hearing about a machine capable of turning musical works into blood-bag beings.

And she drank from the ugliness of his elixir; it was the only thing she could stomach at the time.

She saw weakness where he saw strength (an original phantom menace), and she looked at his arrogant grin, and she wanted to kill that son of a gun.

She was saddened that mercy did not refute violence.

The best way to get everything was to not want anything, but you can't will what you want, so why even try?

She was more burnt out than ever in her current state of affairs. And she asked him if monsters could be tender too.

He was blindsided by his own hypocrisy but could do little to decipher and alleviate the clogged drains of his conscious plumbing.

Her strength was measured by loneliness and uncertainty defined her character. A frightful and beautiful child, a diadem crafted by Hephaestus himself.

And they were in the land of daddy daughters and father mothers.

And she knew that good friends were hard to find but a worthy foe... near impossible.

It was efficiency leaning towards simplicity.

And she decided that she wanted limited houseguests, only those reaped from the muddiness of her own murky roots.

And finally, when she had had enough, she pushed him out the window, and his carcass exploded on the rocks below. And then she cradled her child and sang her her favorite lullaby.

"This is the song that doesn't end. It just goes on and on, my friend."

Chapter 17: The Magician

His name was Andrei, an immaculate magician making the rounds of the medieval world, tent and carriage in tow; he made his mark with sleight-of-hand exaggerations, nifty tricks for the local nitwits, or so he pronounced their mental bearings. He was an inhospitable man, cherishing his ruse with much too much pride and an unseemly and foul pleasure, watching each dumbfounded spectator succumb to his talents with malevolent and condescending glee.

Andrei had been keeping this up for years, circulating his hat for dollars and cents postshow, all the while pickpocketing shortchanging onlookers from the bourgs in forgotten alleyways or even dodgy and sneaky-like lifts amidst the crowded currents of the town square. Of course, he had received his due from time to time. A good beating was part of the job, and as a full-fledged masochist, he saw it as another perk to an already fulfilling and enlightening gig.

It was outside a small village that he met the wee lad. He could have been no more than 7, but his eyes betrayed a fierce cunning, and when the kid spoke, Andrei had great difficulty returning his gaze.

The kid proposed a deal in which he, Timothy, as he proudly proclaimed himself, would show Andrei a trick, and if Andrei could guess how he'd performed the feat, he'd show him a secret passage to Lord Felwhich's chambers, enabling him to sneak in undetected and pillage any gold trinket or valuable artifact he deemed worthy. If he could not, Timothy requested that Andrei relinquish a few shillings.

Andrei hemmed and hawed, less in light of the particularities of the deal and more so because of a nagging suspicion that dearest Timothy was hiding some nasty cards up his tiny sleeves. But he was Andrei, greatest magician in all the land. Fuck this child; he knows not. He is simply an arrogant thing, bewitched by youth, with confidence emanating from some inbred peasant retardation. Fuck this child; we have a deal. He signaled towards Timothy with a nod and a whimsical gesture of his right hand; they had a deal—now let the show begin.

It happened in a flash, from the bushes and overgrown fields, Andrei was rushed by an army of infants or dwarves or tiny children. He couldn't really tell, their fury tantamount to their speed. They accosted him and forced him to yield; he erupted in primal fear and turtled to the ground. He expected to be squashed, lacerated at the bottom of some godforsaken pile; the Great Andrei killed in the fields by some roguish, miniature ghouls. What an end! But as he uncovered himself from his position of refuge, he noticed that it was pitch-black. He was no longer in the fields; he was somewhere else. He looked up and could see what he supposed was the moon, a luminescent orb, but the sensations of what had recently occurred unbalanced him so that he did not seek to elaborate much on the "wheres" and "hows" of his situation; his predicament required balance first, and unfortunately for Andrei, the terrain was not fixed; he found himself on some hellish bog—ebbing and flowing—drunk and mired with confusion with each step.

He met a thing—for a thing is the aptest way of describing it—a monstrous conformation of spherical shapes heaped onto one another. It seemed stuck or rooted in the soil, and it spoke in low groans, with words being unwound and coiled in unfamiliar designations. Andrei asked the beast if it knew where he was. It replied slowly, and Andrei could piece little information from the sounds beyond a significant sense of suffering and disgust that seemed to be accompanying each syllable of the beast's labored speech. He hurriedly went in a haphazardly chosen direction, away from the monstrosity, and he felt the cool air direct his path, led by the wind since his senses seemed to be faltering or, at the very least, distorted to the point of subterfuge.

Down the road, or through the darkness, or whichever way he had been heading, he met a most beautiful woman. She glowed in the darkness and spun a golden shawl through the air landing tentatively on her porcelain shoulders before her next acrobatic jig. Beyond her stunning beauty, Andrei noticed that her face was blurred and clung to the air, congealed and coalescing in the darkness, space combatted with time, distorting and prolonging her elegance—an elegiac ballerina haunting the night sky.

Stranger still, as Andrei approached the woman, she began to sink into the earth, proving her phantasmal qualities once and for all, and Andrei, distraught and dumbfounded, momentarily wished to shed his earthly skin, a quick slash across the gulliver and admittance was sure to follow. But rational turpitude quickly resurfaced, and Andrei decided to leave the pearl unbothered below; he marched on, lost and confused as ever, in no direction in particular.

He then met a large ogre. Loincloth and dangling cock and balls of greenish hues swung in a pendulum-like motion, and Andrei could not avert his gaze, offending the ogre who unstuck a tree from some nearby soil and came panting with angry strides in our hero's frightened direction.

"Shit," he thought, "I've really done it now."

The first swing missed by inches, and Andrei didn't want to allow time for another. He glanced down and noticed, somewhere along the way, unbeknownst to him, he'd acquired a weapon of sorts. A strange-looking rock—tooth-like—like one from a baby mammoth. He wasn't sure how he knew it was a weapon; in reality, it was just an odd-looking rock, but intuitively something stirred when he saw it within his grasp. He raised it, playing show-and-tell with the ogre, who was transfixed by this rare and precious stone.

The dark side of the stone soon shined through as Andrei discovered the violent undercurrent he intuited before. As the ogre gazed, Andrei noticed that its head was beginning to shake and steam was unfurling from its ears. Violent tremors expanded from gentle stutters, and blood began to spew from its eyes, ears, and mouth.

"Shit," thought Andrei, "I've really done it."

Andrei rides out with a souvenir from the dead ogre. He touts its left pinky as a symbol of his victory over his former competitor and vanquished foe. Thoughts circle ideas of reforming the finger as a royal dildo and selling the offending merchandise to Queen Thicket, thorny and debauched libertine and depraved connoisseur of all that was phallic.

But then he was stuck and suddenly sinking. He sees, far off in the distance, an ethereal being, the pearl from yesteryear, come back and resurfaced, waving at him as he descends into her former pit. His turn, by God, and he waves back with exuberant joy; he feels the cool and refreshing welcome of the soil flood and digest his being.

**

Andrei woke up to a large and less than ordinary field, alone, spread-eagle, money and hat missing, large bump on the cranium, kid gone, and cart and tent nowhere to be found. "Christ," he thought, "fucking Timothy." He rubbed his eyes and patted the bump on his head and surveyed his locale. Squinting, he made out a group of young females foraging for wild carnivorous mushrooms, or so it appeared, and alongside the described damsels was a large-scale game of lavish croquet being played by some aristocratic sorts in odd maquillage. A lone dubiously striped tent stood at the far end of the field, functioning as an apothecary for the roaming athletes, and Andrei walked in its direction in search of a viable remedy for his splitting headache.

Chapter 18: The Marriage

Two dreamers compete for the title of All-Powerful Builder. Whose consciousness will prevail and ascend to the top rank? Stay tuned, dear reader, and remember the clues, all answers lie beyond the world of words, and he who builds in the foreground will often have a long and rickety crack in the foundation of his creation.

Her mouth is agape. A slight stream of drool seeps down the crease to the right of her chin. Soft rumbles with a hint of influx reverberate, summoning out the rhythms of her breath. She's an angel with halitosis. He pushes his body close to hers and tries to match her state. Slow it down, enter her dreams, head against pillow—1... 2... 3...

***

It started out the same way it does for everyone. One amiable mass of flesh and muscle attracted to another.

He sat her down and spoke carefully. It came out just above a whisper, and the muted syllables expressed a parasitic love devoid of humiliation and glory.

She liked it best when they sat together on cold nights and watched the television set.

At 35, she was as stunning as ever. Yoga workshops and aerobics classes were keeping her fit and trim, and he found the slight sag and softening of her vivacious body alluring and less intimidating.

An hour before he died, he was staring at a flower bed for no particular reason.

They had three children who brought them lots of joy and a few disappointments.

He never figured any of it out.

She baked pies on Sunday; he cut the wood.

He was struck by the similarities between thinking every 1's a piece of shit and every 1's equal.

2+2 could be 4.

She did not resent any of it, although she thought of it as a mostly sad and lonely affair.

He needed to accumulate or destroy. She needed to attack or retreat.

She asked him about his day as she always did. An offering of idiosyncrasies underlying his routine answers. Small, automated, foolproof. He checked his eyes in the mirror, washed his hands in the sink, and brushed his teeth with a dry toothbrush.

Left over right. North over south.

She loved the pattern and dance of a well-orchestrated flock.

And he told her about the boy who shot the other boy for no reason at all.

***

He loved her more than she loved him.

Their next-door neighbor was a cretin.

She measured well on the social barometer.

He was all politics and pageantry.

Their best moments were tender and sporadic, sandwiched between silliness and sensuality.

His penis measured a mark below six inches, and his height was a touch above six feet.

She thought mastery meant more from less.

The fact that he didn't believe in much absolved him of certain sins.

In principle, she was against lying for personal gain.

His happiest moments involved cartoons on a television screen.

She craved irrevocable change.

And nostalgia plagued him from the very beginning.

He drove her to the diner as they did each and every Sunday. He looked at her and smiled. She could feel his gaze and opted to keep her own pointed out the passenger window.

Hills of billowing snow, black skies, zigzagging winds.

The radio played an outdated country song, and they both hummed along as the streetlights counted perfect time, a visual metronome to their eastbound journey.

As he walked across the snow-covered field, he cursed the wind and yelled, "The wind is a cunt."

Chapter 19: Debbie

E.

"Get your mincemeat dick away from me, you miserable old kike." E. stormed off and slammed the front door, meeting Debbie downstairs in a heated rage on the first-floor landing. As they exited the apartment lobby, she heard yells from the floors above, a mishmash of acoustic resonance and indecipherable consonant and vowel pairings. Mr. Klink's own verbose rebuttal was making its way along the apartment passage, muddled and distorted en route.

Debbie: What happened?

E. told her the tale and described the scenario. The perverted old chap had unsheathed his penis while E. played "Prelude in E Minor."

The piano teacher's semi-hard schlong... an uninvited interlocutor to the lesson... E., petite schoolgirl... shocked and disturbed... ran out surprised by the gall of her elderly instructor.

Debbie: You know he's not Jewish, right?

E. told her brothers about the incident, and they promised retribution for their 15-year-old sister. Their youthful exuberance had found a moral cause, exacerbated by their already malignant demeanors, and they promised swift and vengeful justice.

When Debbie saw Mr. Klink again at a local fast-food joint, he looked no worse for wear. Although E. had detailed to Debbie the exploits of her brothers—"smashed kneecaps" and "grating barbed wire"—she saw no evidence of any assault. His gait remained stiff and slow; his skin was sunken and discolored—a man weathered by age, broken by time, not shattered by baseball bats. She wished him a piss-poor pot of pure bad luck and took off down the street before he caught sight of her.

Three weeks later, her mom told her of Mr. Klink's ill fortune.

Mom: Apparently, he'd been trying to move... truck parked... slipped back... brake failure... crushed against the wall... stuck... brutalized... 12 hours... alone... severe pain... died at daybreak... sad... piano teacher... survivor... horrible end.

Debbie didn't know what to think; Mr. Klink was dead. The hand of God had seen fit to allow his truck to roll back on him, put an end to his terrestrial doings once and for all. Debbie felt a pang sear her side. She could not decide on the proper emotive course, strange feelings arose from contradictory points, a sonata developed from the strings of her stomach. She ached with unsettled rawness and sat confused at the mercy of the gastric violinist, a virtuoso puppet master playing motive against motive, building layers of depraved complexity in the dogged pit of poor Debbie's gut.

Examples cited sexual deviancy and pedophilia as karmic indicators favoring the positive nature of the event, but Debbie's doubts were not altogether assuaged by this reasoning. Memories of Mr. Klink playing piano at neighborhood parties and jesting kindly with a benevolent air made it difficult to cast him as the outright manifestation of monstrous evil. And then there was his death, the common denominator, nature's dinner bell, life's treacherous equalizer residing in its endnote, central to its balance, founded on equality, for the good and the bad alike, Republican and Democrat, saint and pedophile, summed up as a dubious sayonara uniting all mankind. Had he suffered enough in his final frames to deserve more than sheer disgust at the utterance of his name? Or was his legacy to be uprooted by the truth, conniving deviant that he was? Debbie's heart hurt, and she welcomed the comfort of watching a Disney flick with her younger sister, Trisha.

At the funeral, Debbie noticed E. crying quietly, tucked away in the back near her mother. Debbie sought her out after the service, curious of her state, both as an inquisitive friend and a selfish benefactor, eager to understand her own feelings through a lens closer to the flame than her own.

V.

Dream #1: (esophagus, snake, log 'n' snow, boy with wire, electrode, taunt, malicious smile. He says: Treat your enemies as friends and your friends as enemies.)

The ultimate dismissal of morality as fabrication for minute timeframes, unimportant to the overarching and uninhibited cosmic chaos of the infinite.

Although time may not heal all wounds, it will inevitably forget them.

(The deity does not deign to show the design.)

Style was the measure of a man, and morality was all but a third of the equation.

"Right," she says. "Isn't that right?"

"My renegade rights think elsewise," says the dove in the back in the purple gown.

"A blindworm listens, and revenge was just the ticket."

"The most callous crime was reflecting truth back at the unarmed (1-armed) fool."

A mongoloid midget with buckteeth gets kicked for rubbing his genitals on a gentleman in a posh clothing-store lineup.

News Headline

That bitch lost all her money and bitched about it all the way home.

Based On A True Story

A slithering snake slides southbound along arterial lines, a gastric tube of digestive menace seeking a sentient source of supper. It knows not mercy or cruelty and reacts with stubborn intuition at the sight of poor little Cindy T., sitting alone among the bedrock of an old isle.

She leveled the gun and fired at the approaching car. The high school lovers—two sophomore sweethearts—collapsed simultaneously into each other's arms, a bloody mess as seen through the shattered pulp of a Cadillac Eldorado windshield.

It's important to derail the train sometimes... abruptly wakes up.

O.

The mirror maker knows that the trick to any good mirror lies in the artfulness in which it displays its tiny, minute flaw. A grotesque tweak, a slight bend, a poetic exaggeration to ensnare the viewer, trapping them in their most primitive and myopic narcissism, ripping and churning the stomach, an exorcism under beauty's elixir, the ideal anesthetic to alleviate the body's modern malaise.

1. Pit sword against foe
2. Add retribution through rebirth
3. Land infamy among an army of morons
4. Strike with guile and wit
5. Rinse and repeat

Is it better to act badly under false pretenses with sincere motives?

Is it better to endure and ignore?

Is the guarded innocence of another worth the self-sacrifice?

If timelessness is the goal, which moral lens clarifies the hostilities of the perpetrator?

Is punishment rectifying and pain the payment, or is endurance the sentence and time the executioner?

There is a pedophile on stage. A single overhead light illuminates him from above. He sits in a wooden chair, uncomfortable and rigid. The audience is all women. They are silent, then begin to whisper, a wave of growth is upon them. The pedophile is nervous but doesn't move and remains unsettled below the overhead light. The crickets chirp loudly, and the audience is now deafening. A woman stands up. She is veiled in a crown of darkness, and the crowd hushes. She excuses herself and exits her pew and walks towards the stage. She is wearing a black dress cut above the knee with an old-fashioned pillbox hat. She proceeds towards center stage and enters the light. She bows to the crowd who remain silent. She reaches below her dress and into her underwear and produces a small Walther PPK pistol. She aims at the pedophile and discharges the weapon. He screams milliseconds before the first shots are fired and goes limp shortly thereafter. She fires again, and his corpse dances in short bursts against the pistol pops. She drops the gun and turns to the crowd and says, "Now, what should we talk about?"

"Is life lived in a glasshouse?"

L.

When asked a question about modern beauty, the suitor answered, "Beauty is a balance of exaggerations; a craftsman's exposé of the interior workspaces on display in the uniform of the proprietor's choosing. It is beautiful because it is right, and it is right because it is beautiful. We sense it instinctively, an implicit arousal of our most primitive sentiments towards truth. Its mastery succeeds beyond time, where songs are most harmonious, elusive, and dangerous."
—couturier

"One must scrub away the grime of its time, delouse the false demigods and descend into cryptic pits with malfunctioning flashlights. There, beauty is most apt to rest; she seeks her counterpoint. There among the putrid and the prodigal, the tender lily sleeps."

—sculptress or garbage woman

The tragedy of their time centered on their worship of the word—a gauche attempt to cleanse speech of its haughtiness, an aspiring egalitarian language of idiots, the Babylonian curse striving towards destruction.

He saw it and was disgusted by it. Twinkling in the man's eye, he could see the uncontrolled desire, the malfunctioning urge superseding all others, the rift, pushing him towards domination at any cost. George asked the creep if he'd leave her alone. To which he replied, "Maybe, maybe not."

After the trials, John's ego was reduced to a small heap of asinine pebbles, diamonds cut from the rubble, valuable in the world's avaricious eyes but certainly not worth their weight. Disappointing diamonds... the rarest sort.

The world could not touch her passion. It resided deep within her, clubbed and beaten, misunderstood and spat upon; it was her faith that pushed her forward, one menial step at a time.

She hated with impunity. She hated their lies, their righteousness, their inability to see the futility, causing malignant destruction again and again, all in the name of some supposed *virtue-du-jour*. The fad that galvanized the troops once more, called forth the actors, seedlings of destruction, drunk on morals and providence. The idiots marched on, a sickly sight for anyone capable of recognizing the common and debased beat to which they so heartily clung.

And a bomb goes off, and a woman is raped, and a young boy gets cancer, and the sour world turns once more.

She dreamt a lot of underground pools.

His only options were those of the abhorrent moralist or the constant gardener.

"Life is a crude, uncouth dance of unabridged fuckups and folly, aligned with the grace of a good laugh and a spectacular decapitation every so often."

—Blue Moon

&

They abduct them in their dreams and in open alleyways, tumors with erect cattle prods, agents of subterranean disarray, and a painful reminder that all is not right with the world and probably never will be.

And (in) the darkness of their dreams (it) was pure suspiria.

E.

A path forgoing the slow and sensible in favor of the swift and sharp.

The neophyte began to speak with loud candor and senseless vigor. Debbie couldn't take it anymore and kicked that son of a bitch in the testes. He buoyed about before finally toppling over. When Jen asked why she'd attacked the poor bastard, she replied, "He said she was lying, and a tasteless statement like that deserves vengeance."

It was difficult not to gain momentum in light of the stakes. The culture was divided by extremes and bound to entice animosity from both ends for wildly different reasons. Ideas of justice, virtue, and self-preservation were flung around haphazardly, hell-bent on destroying the crude arguments opposing their own infantile demands.

Debbie sat at the fast-food restaurant and drank her Coke. It was spring now; E. had left on a sailing trip to the Galapagos—a maritime adventure before she started school in the fall. Debbie eyed the budding trees and the happy-go-lucky families entering the eatery with jovial panache but couldn't quite register why she felt excluded from their joy. She felt bound to an instinct aroused recently, befuddled by the Mr. Klink mess and now the absent E.

She met him walking her dog, ice cream cone in hand. He made her laugh and was rude and mean with kindness slipping through an anxious smile. She called him a dork, and she adored him, and he cherished her.

Her dog's name was Corb, and he sang with beautiful, savage colors.

(He struts wildly with brazen uncertainty.)

Debbie and Glen (senior by 1 year) walked hand in hand along the lakeshore. He stared into her eyes and told her he loved her and spoke of amorous urges, citing a passionate inkling leaning towards destruction, bashing her brains in with his Little League baseball bat, and she responded in kind, saying she wished to cut off his johnson with her dollar-store scissors. They laughed loudly, and the gawking strangers smiled at their blossoming, idiosyncratic love.

The lovebirds continued their walk, but an aggressive outburst postponed their intimate *rencontre*. A homeless man was yelling at the mailbox; propping open the slot, he yelled obscenities at the letters below. His salivary glands pumped reams of spittle upon helpless letters who were now forced to carry a load of the man's DNA globetrotting to unsuspecting recipients, contaminating unknown numbers of eager, well-to-do fingers, which might unwittingly touch innocent, well-to-do lips, which could presumably smear and kiss and infect ignorant and well-to-do lovers. They would all fall prey to this third-party hijack, spreading this rampant conspiracy at a seismic rate, all through no fault of their own.

They would often mute the TV and view the silent segments with a detached aura, siphoning away the historical recourse. Judging each action by the merit of its immediacy and the primal reactions it evoked. A deranged sense of truth emerged from these viewings.

He had balls of diamonds and a prick of steel.

She asked for advice while she fellated him. He said, "Just be yourself and don't fucking stop."

Perfecting is a solitary endeavor, and so they decided to each go their own separate way, and their mental worlds grew expansive.

Debbie missed Glen, but deep in her heart of hearts, she preferred the silence of her solo adventuring. She ran into him from time to time, and he'd relinquish his exuberant and natural air the moment he caught sight of her. He said loud and stupid things for her to overhear, and when she left, he followed her with a saddened and remorseful gaze.

Could one be benevolent through their malevolence? Debbie's mind pondered Qs such as these which produced no veritable As, but ripe fruit clung to these pursuits nonetheless. She was the knight of medieval meanderings, a conquistador in search of an oasis of truth. A warrior with a bloodied axe and a hyperactive meat mass calling itself "The Brain."

They were magicians in the ashes, and a stone tablet whispered:

"You lonely, soot-filled soul,
You lame and sullen queen,

Rise up from the garbage dump,
And devour your Dionysian dream."

Some say their virtue was hidden in their beauty, and style was a modern demon.

Everyone was getting hard and wet, and there were a lot of juices in the stew, and everyone was competing for the proverbial heart. It was filled with delirium and had a succulent and savory taste. A real dreamer's dish.

V.

Dream #2: (I wish people would start smoking instead of jumping off bridges, or the nobility of silence.)

To be terribly observant was a true curse, and the card read, "I want to tear out your heart and eat it. Love, John."

She kept him on the sidewalk for a long time, and a red hand blinked rapidly at him from across the way.

And he thought, "The best drugs are cerebral and lethargic."

She masticated her grub and micturated in the john and drank up her cup of joe.

They were the seasick sailors silently upchucking on the bow of the ship with eyes gazing starboard towards hopeful horizons.

And the stone tablet said, "Everything leaves a stain."

And her last instinct was one of survival.

When he said, "Writing was a smoker's curse," she realized that she had flawless technique but was weak as hell.

It took some years for him to lose his vulgar disposition, but in the end, he came out all right.

He was a bombastic and squirrelly fuck, and he tried to

understand the women of his life by classifying them according to their gel and shellac nails.

She enjoyed the wolves at the door but only those whose style accommodated her own cannibalistic and predatory disposition.

Backwards and forwards, they understood that it was best to work in indirect routes, and it was good to look forward to that which the others feared and strayed from, as it made you the genuine article, a real horrorshow sight, and it gave off an air of unconquerable dignity.

But it was unacceptable by most standards except she couldn't shake her inherent interest pulling her towards it. It was beauty down in the dumps—guttural beauty—the real McCoy.

And the castaway sailor just floated for a while, stranded and staring up at the bright blue sky as sharks circled underneath.

I.

The Nazi soldier stomped hard, bringing his knee above his hip and mechanically coming down on the poor *devotchka*'s head. In a matter of minutes, the village had become overrun with Third Reich militants, sloshing their galoshes through the muddied soil; someone yells something that sounds like, "I gots no time!"

He would allow his soul the choice—psycho or saint, yet to be determined—and grin and bear the outcome.

Salvation in solitude, not in the shackles of some stilted mass morality.

And it was all a matter of how much chaos a soul could take before madness bore in to support it.

They were the modern priests drawn towards interpretation; undaunted by their lack of courage, they sought strength in numbers; warriors inebriated by a loud and powerful voice proclaiming justice and virtue for all, so long as they indoctrinate their youth and castrate the oddballs.

The Nazis criticized the boy for his choice of undergarments and promptly blew off his head.

And sometimes I have bad days, he thought.

L.

She looked around and noticed that they all had mouths and assholes. And she saw them as detestable creatures, origins in inebriated dick slime.

Her communication with the others was restricted to an esoteric means of symbolism. Grunts and tongue clacks were submitted alongside guttural howls in the absence of anything better. Language was at its dawn, full of enigmatic links and confusing loops, an abstruse game of cat's cradle for the early *Homo sapiens* mind.

They sat outside the cave midway up the mountain; flames licked skyward, and ash beat down against the rancor of their brow. They were seven, huddled around the fire, and she began her tale with the clack of her tongue, and the intensity of the diatribe was not lost on her primitive mates.

Click... hum... burp... whistle... moo... bing... tongue swish... gurgle... gurgle... (straw-like sucking)... rapturous wails... back to moos... more swishing... some strange movement + clockwise head circles and low-note humming... blah, blah, "Donner Party," meow, loud kiss... incoherent murmur... speaking in tongues... catch words like "muse, Bentley, Easter, sick, new order," catch other words like "pig, swindle, time, New Year, coke, waffle, machete, minx."

And she hijacked their rhythm, for she was a gifted and natural storyteller.

Full translation of the above text, along with the rest of the text and the incidents which followed, was carefully translated into modern English by the proud linguists and translators of the University of Hillcrest, Memphis.

The story goes…

In their quest for perfection, they blew up the world.

And one of the men asked her how she told such wondrous and interesting stories, and she said that she thought of her stories as movies and first worked them out as scripts. Then she would work them out as pictures, and then she'd edit the sequences or pictures or clips together. Then, when she was happy with the movie, she would start to think of the stories as songs and make sure the tone was right, and then she would think of them as one long drum solo served up by a gifted musician but one who was self-taught and came with baggage and was a little bit deaf. And finally, she would think of them as meals, with a serving of meat, some hearty carbohydrates, and a bunch of bright and lush vegetables. She said that sometimes she snuck some poison into the meals, but that was only on very special occasions.

And she said, "That's how I spin my web and/or build my house."

And they took comfort in the insignificance of it all. And they wondered, "Which illusions were in vogue today?"

And they called upon the recipe of the stars to illuminate their wisdom, and they sang their hymns and bedded down near a steep cliff and sank into stupor near the smolder of the campfire.

That night one of the men dreamt of the moon. He dreamt of it in three phases. The first of which depicted it suddenly, appearing out of nowhere, surprising him, the dreamer, as it were, and it came closer and was denser than he had ever seen before. It was beautiful, but there was an underlying sense of danger in the enormity of its image, as if the moon were a threatening force, like a beautiful mare, posturing and proud, daring the onlooker into some sort of common duel. The next bit began with a loud crack; he was conversing with someone in the dream and a loud sound like thunder or an exploding car, a mighty and deafening noise—crack—and he looked up and saw the moon rotating only a hundred or so feet over- head, circling so near the earth that its collision was surely imminent. He could see vast craters as it rotated above, and his feelings of terror and beauty were multiplied tenfold.

He had trouble remembering the third part, which was the actual collision when the moon had finally struck the earth, but what came after, the aftermath, he remembered perfectly well. He was in a parking lot surrounded by large buildings that looked like a university campus, and he was trapped, and the moon and the destroyed buildings coalesced together into some architectural fusion of marble tapestries and alien rock, and no one knew how to get out of this sci-fi fever dream or where anything was or where the exits were because no one had ever been there before. And it was a completely new structure that still held some of the elegance of its former bearings but was now dressed in sinister and otherworldly vibes.

The dreamer woke to screams and yells and opened his eyes to see one of the men kicking the woman who had earlier told them the tale. "This bitch has poisoned my mind," he yelled. "She's a witch," and he continued to kick her, and she coughed up blood, and the others rushed over to her defense but not before the maniac had had his way with her. And the maniac ranted and cursed them all and spat upon the helpless heap of a woman. The others stared, stunned, breathing heavily, but before they could get any words out, he vanished into the darkness, descending the mountain in large, aggressive strides.

In the morning, the man who dreamt of the moon offered to carry the woman on his back during the day's ascent of the mountain. She declined. Her face was badly beaten, and she had to stop often during the day to spit blood and rest, and her left arm seemed to be stuck to her side, and her movements were rigid and slow.

As they climbed, the man remembered more and more of his dream, and he remembered that while he was trapped by the moon in the ruins of the structure he went wandering underground, and there—somewhere among the rubble—he found a hidden fortune; although he couldn't remember where or what the fortune was, he was certain it was valuable or invaluable or held some form of magic and was, at the very least, an important archeological find.

"*There's a world worth fighting for, and it's a most violent and heinous and brutal world, and it usurps the most tender and beautiful, and vice versa.*"

When she reached the summit, she was no longer alone, a stray dog accompanied her, as her former companions had long ago withdrawn, some into careless pursuits tailored to their weaknesses, chaining them in bourgeois decorum with pimples in their cheeks and diabetes in their bones, while others were blown from the cliffs by unfortunate storms and unexpected gusts of wind, and yet others were taken in by the throes of insanity and vertigo.

The dog had met her near the peak, and its good-natured bark had brought tears to her eyes.

She watched the stars and drank in the cool mountainous air, and on the third day, she cut the dog's throat and roasted it on the fire. Its meat was succulent, but she was sorry she had to travel so far down the rabbit hole.

And she refilled her cup with a half-half mixture of silence and solitude.

It was a simple story of a wide array of animals surviving in an ever-changing climate.

It was also the story of a centipede who wanted to be a butterfly and a love letter to the universe and an advisory about rapidly changing weather.

Chapter 20: Duane

The gladiator swung his axe, and the crowd went fucking nuts. All the while, a lone ant scampers across the desert terrain scouting for provisions for his fellow comrades. These two episodes run concurrently, but neither is aware of the other's existence. Both occupy the same arena within the same time-frame, and each story is concerned with survival with each occupant in dire straits if their dangers are not bested. The ant and the gladiator. An unassuming solidarity veiled in a cloud of narcissism and ignorance. The brutes fight on, gunning for more time under the chill of their own limited perspectives.

(Beyond this paragraph, the struggle of the ant will go no further, as its story has an abrupt and all-too-familiar end in which it succumbs to its injuries, squashed under the boot of some large foreign mammal.)

He judged others by a simple criterion based on whether they grew quieter or louder with age.

A young nurse falls in love with Ms. Miller, who's admitted to the hospital and diagnosed with a strange parasitic disease.

The nurse sits patiently, tending to her ailment, doing her best to aid Ms. Miller and deliver her from her suffering. But alas, the disease seems to hold the upper hand, and with each new medical advancement in her case, another negative side effect sprouts its head. The disease embodies the myth of the Hydra, and at a loss to define it, the doctors go about calling it "The Phantom," and its presence surrounds the hospital and sends dark waves rippling with disillusionment, debunking the grandeur of the greatest medical minds and leaving a general sense of malaise and helplessness in its wake.

The discombobulated hospital is located a quarter mile from the coliseum where the gladiator's matches take place, and the dead ant lies entrenched in the sand.

Beneath the coliseum—in the subterranean heart of the edifice—lies a jail containing many captives, the most notable are the nefarious clan dubbed "The Nectors." A family of rural cannibals caught only recently by local law enforcement.

"I am the goddamn paterfamilias, and I've chosen my daemon," spoke the crooked-tooth dandy by the name of Walter Lee Nector. "*Hear ye, hear ye*. His hooves approacheth."

The Nectors had decided to raise hell (in both a literal and figurative sense); the cannibal captives sought the aid of the demon known as Duane. An oddball creature whose earliest known reference dates back to roughly 150 BC when a Roman soldier named Germanicus caught sight of the creature after a glorious victory over Hermann and the barbarous German horde.

All the while, as Walter Lee worked on the conjuring ritual, little Bobby Sue thought back to the last delectable meal he'd eaten. A young man he'd met at the market who'd shown signs of outright indignation and volatile mischief. He cried loudly about poorly developed pears and inedible turnips to the vendors, throwing a hissy fit and loudly putting on a deranged show in order to gratify his own false sense of misaligned superiority. Bobby Sue had taken him in an alleyway, stabbing him in quick jabs to incapacitate him, then flaying him and strategically taking his kidneys and pancreas while leaving the rest to rot in the sun. He cooked his organs with vegetables from the market and paired them with a nice half-liter of wine.

As if their tongues had new masters, the Nectors, in unison, in the darkness of their cell, began to speak. Each in turn reverberated the chorus, "Fire is coming, fire is coming, fire is coming..." But this actually sounded like "tik-fook-scuffitits" because of their dialect and because they were missing some crucial teeth.

And then there was the sacrifice, something Walter Lee had failed to mention to the rest of his clan. He knew that his family would not approve but that its necessity was paramount. During the night, with a broken pane of glass, he cut his youngest daughter's throat. He silenced her with as much swiftness and mercy as his strike could warrant. His eyes welled up with tears, and he turned away from the young corpse knowing that the hardest part was over. He steadied himself, then dug the knife inside his shoulder and sliced with fervor and violence at the entanglement of tissue comprising his left arm.

They were all screaming when his limb came undone and fell to the floor, and then all the lights went out.

When Walter Lee first met Duane, he thought he looked defiantly ordinary, except, of course, for his eyes and ears. They betrayed a fierce cunning, one whose origin began in the most tepid and indifferent of fires.

"Everyone betrays themselves if you look closely enough."

While the Nectors were summoning their demon god, the city was caught in the perils of a developing epidemic. The first signs of the plague arose from an unaccountable manifestation of dead frogs suddenly appearing all over the urban landscape. They would hop in an ordinary fashion and then, out of the blue, start to gyrate and shuffle, popping like kernels of corn, and finally toppling over, dead as a doornail. Their death throes sounded like an inhaled *ribbit*, and a new organization was commissioned and sanctioned by the Senate in order to rid the city of these sprawled-out amphibian corpses.

Ms. Miller died two weeks after being admitted to the hospital, and our young heroine nurse was heartbroken at the loss. She wasn't sure why she'd felt such affection for Ms. Miller, their words had been few, and their time rather brief, yet a void had developed in her at their parting, and she felt a shift in her persona, a realigned trajectory a couple of degrees from its prior course. A small adjustment with big consequences.

"The Phantom," or what doctors later referred to as "The Frog Plague," grew tenfold after the death of Ms. Miller, she being the first victim of this mysterious and deadly disease to have been admitted to the hospital. Over the course of the next week, 50 patients with similar symptoms were admitted, and all perished within a fortnight of their arrival. The week after that, over 800 new plague-stricken patients were admitted, and a special quarantined ward was developed for the victims of the so-called "Frog Plague" in the ruins of an old army barracks. By the end of the month, a total of 5,647 patients were admitted, all contenders in a losing battle with the eponymous tetrapod disease, and a state of emergency was declared.

The great plague was making its sweep across the land, and it overturned their lives, locking them in a dire loop, mocking tragedy by corroding it with monotony, deflating death, and rendering their lives vacant and seemingly obsolete. Repetition and rapid exits had poisoned the well, and they only recognized their predicament much too late.

"Color me hopeless."

There stood an old diseased tree near the center of town that took on the role of unofficial mascot in the time of pestilence.

Now back to the Nectors... they stayed cooped up in their cell with the addition of the demon known as Duane as the plague was wreaking havoc above. Duane hypnotized the guards and cast a spell altering his appearance, cloaking him in what appeared to be the guise of the Nectors' youngest daughter, Jeanne. Upon entering the cell, as a form of payment to the Nectors, he evaporated the body of the young girl, although he left Walter Lee's severed arm, which they in turn used as raw nourishment for their upcoming escapades. Biding their time, they lay in wait.

During the plague and the demon summoning and all that other jazz, the gladiator continued his series of victories, accumulating a total of 15 decapitations and 23 disembowelments during the month of May. He pledged his victories to the gods of Mars and drank heavily, overflowing with joy at his own invincibility.

"6 days compete for the title of Best in Show." This is what Duane told them. Although his advice often seemed nonsensical, he had a way of captivating their attention, partly because he'd decided to adopt the appearance of Jeanne, the youngest Nector daughter, on a more permanent basis; his actual appearance, or what they assumed was his actual appearance, seemed more like a giant nightmarish hare mixed with the proportions of an athletic, if not slender, middle-aged man. On the 5th day, they broke out of the underground prison.

A thought coming from the mind of the newly released Mrs. Jolene Kassidy Nector, wife of Walter Lee Nector: "When he used to suck the lint from my toes and barricade his schnoz in my armpits... was that when he loved me most?"

In this tale, there is also a man who goes by the nickname Dogman. He is an uncharacteristically coarse and vile human being in the eyes of most of the city's inhabitants. He spends most of his time in the public eye howling and drunk on concoctions of his own making. He seems unbothered in the time of the plague and is the only citizen yet to be transformed by the madness circulating around town. Others may pretend that all is well, ignore the looming signs of distress felt and glimpsed at every street corner, but suppressed or repressed, they still know the truth, and it shapes and chisels away at their core. But not Dogman—he sits unfazed—howling like before, drunk and barking and enjoying the enigma of rare elixirs and beautiful intoxicants unleashed in their quintessence and flowering to their greatest potency in times of danger and imminent doom.

When the Nectors, along with Duane (or Jeanne), resurfaced into the world, the first thing Jeanne did was walk over to a sickly old woman who'd recently been infected with the plague and spit on her. People were aghast at the little girl, spitting and defiling an old invalid. Where had the youth's respect gone? thought the passersby. One woman was so affronted that she grabbed Jeanne and asked her what sort of devil would spit on an old woman. Jeanne replied that she'd cured her, and to the woman's amazement, she had.

Word of Jeanne and her miracle spittle quickly spread throughout the city. She was paraded around, an arsenal of saliva disinfecting the metropolis. She was praised as a god and a true redeemer. In less than two weeks, she had singlehandedly rid the city of the plague. People made a religious spectacle out of her curing methods; an awe-inspiring silence surrounded her as she puckered her mouth, readying the release of her celebrated fluid, the onlookers mute, except, of course, for Dogman, who roared with laughter each and every time he witnessed the spectacle, and when asked what he found so funny about the curing of the sick and the extinguishing of pain and suffering, he howled louder with laughter, never able to articulate a proper reply.

The Nectors were given a parade and a full pardon for their past atrocities and wrongdoings. Even some of the relatives of those they had eaten showed up for the festivities. They publicly took an oath swearing allegiance and civil obedience to the state and claimed to be under new dietary restrictions. They crossed their hillbilly fingers while making the above-mentioned claims and were—no doubt—as evil as ever, even if the mob thought otherwise and (temporarily) adored their murdering little hearts.

When one of the townsfolk asked Jeanne how she knew her spit was the cure, and why she decided to spit on the old woman first, she replied, "The monster in my spaghetti factory told me so."

The adventure continues until it doesn't...

The Nectors held weekly sermons in which Jeanne preached her holy word, and the populace came to lend their ears and, afterwards, air their grievances, and Jeanne—acting as the presiding judge in a civil court—would bestow her verdict and all parties would abide the young messiah's ruling. The Nectors had somehow usurped most of the governmental bodies in the city; they (senators and such)—still in awe of the little miracle spitter—were too afraid and thankful as of yet to seek the power back. These sermons and sessions of arbitration held sway over the populace. Not to mention the fact that she always finished her sermons with a live show, a magician working a miracle whereby she'd cure one lucky incurable case, from blindness to leprosy; she'd orchestrate a great gob of saliva and let it buck in the face of the soon-to-be healed. They—dripping with spittle—would begin to cry and prostrate themselves at Jeanne's feet.

When asked about vengeance—an eye for an eye, a tooth for a tooth—its cascading and multiplying effect, an explosion, or a great bubonic surge, she shrugged apathetically and said, "Well, if you don't want the world to explode, then don't kick me."

All the while, the gladiator was disenchanted with the new state of things. Yes, the plague had been eradicated, and many hundreds, if not thousands, were saved, but he'd lost much of his crowd. Even in times of disease and degradation, the seats used to be filled, but now that Jeanne was in town, the messiah and miracle worker, the city's appetite for violence had waned. He was not accustomed to this lack of attention; even the vendors had ceased to offer him deals on his favorite cuts of meat. He decided to take matters into his own hands. Had the Nectors not been a clan of villains, thieves, murderers, and cannibals only a few weeks before? Could he not harken the populace's memories back to those days and perhaps prompt Walter Lee to a duel, chop off his other arm, leave him the helpless fool that the gladiator knew he was?

When the gladiator came head-to-head with the Nectors, it was in the middle of the town square. He was carrying his most prized weapon—a large metallic axe—and the Nectors eyed him with suspicion. He vocalized his resentment against the Nectors and listed some of their more memorable and atrocious crimes from their pre-plague days, and then he challenged Walter Lee to a duel and conceded to wearing a blindfold in order to even the odds against the one-armed cannibal.

Walter Lee accepted the challenge, thinking that Jeanne or Duane would protect him. The fight begins: a circle is cleared in the square for the combatants. The gladiator's eyes are bound, and Walter Lee is given a sword from a nearby guard. They circle each other, and the gladiator— using his ears alone—lunges forward at his adversary. Jeanne, watching, decides to employ none of her powers; Walter Lee has been annoying her lately; he, forgetting that she's actually an all-powerful demon, has begun to treat her like his actual daughter—and Duane, or Jeanne, decides that this is as good a time as any to teach Walter Lee a lesson. The crowd is aghast as Walter Lee screams and is rendered armless by a quick and decisive swing from the gladiator's axe.

Jeanne decided to intercede at this point, seeing as the crowd had recovered from its shock and were now tantalized and hypnotized by their old pal bloodshed, moving their favor in the direction of the gladiator. Jeanne stepped forward and signaled the gladiator to remove his blindfold. She then told him to kneel before her; he laughed, and the crowd accompanied his sentiment. Jeanne then snapped her fingers, and all the bones in the gladiator's lower extremities bent and contorted in the most unnatural of angles, rendering his cries of agony the sole audible commotion in an otherwise mute and dumbfounded environment.

He got what he asked for, and it was worse than anything he could have ever imagined.

The gladiator dragged himself across the rugged city terrain and out into the darkened forest; he fastened splints from broken branches and did his best to reposition his bones in some semblance of their former placement. In the aftermath of his defeat and his immobilized state, he swore vengeance against the Nectors, tossing away any morsel of empathy or love he may have fostered in the pits of his heart. His eyes rewarded now bore the cataracts of a vile beast, and the languages of man ceased to operate in the foundations of his soul.

After Walter Lee's second appendage was severed, Jeanne decided to leave him in this helpless state at least for a little while. She summoned a local nurse to care for Walter Lee in their large 5-bedroom abode. Jeanne asked for the most gifted and caring nurse presently employed at the hospital, and, dear savvy reader, can you guess whose soft pitter-patter footsteps ascended the manor's front porch?

The young nurse—the empathetic caregiver from before whose radiance and goodwill shone for even the most imbecilic to notice—entered the Nectors' house and was shown the aging cannibal who'd been wrapped and bandaged in a parody of proper medical etiquette. The young nurse unwrapped, then rewrapped him, and soothed his troubles as best she could with her calm and hushed cadence, although Walter Lee, ashamed and angered at his current predicament, found in the young nurse the perfect sub-missive target to heap his bile onto. Jeanne watched the acidic tirade as Walter Lee cursed and spit at the poor young caregiver, and Jeanne decided that she'd leave Walter Lee as is—in his current impaired state—for a long while yet. Fuck that asshole, she thought. She also thought that the young nurse was one of the most beautiful persons she'd ever seen, and as quickly as Cupid's arrow could force its way into the hardened hide of an overgrown mongrel-hare-cum-demon, Jeanne felt the first pangs of love interpose in her depths.

When Walter Lee asked Duane if he thought there was any chance for a no-armed fat man to be happy in today's world, Duane replied, "You are in a hall of mirrors, and you ask the only asshole." Walter Lee pressed on for a less nonsensical answer to his query, but the demon only replied with statements such as, "People always sell their madness too cheaply," and, "You must kill what you were to become what you ought to be," and finally, "You are hare-by invited to the prestigious duck and goose soirée, but beware the seats; they have appetites which exceed your own."

There are pages missing in the original manuscript, an abbreviated summary of the events follows:

Jolene Kassidy Nector gets jealous of nurse;

Walter Lee falls in love with nurse, too.

(Anger and pride masking his actual feelings.)

Jolene tries to kill and eat nurse.

Duane (or Jeanne) saves nurse, and they escape into the dark forest.

They meet the broken gladiator—repair and heal him (doesn't know who they are (Duane disguises himself as a generic-looking fella))—they send the gladiator back in tip-top shape; he says something like, "Color me sold," and he goes back to the city.

Duane and the nurse leave in the opposite direction and head west.

Gladiator returns and kills all the Nectors.

10 years later, Duane and the nurse return back to the city.

Someone says something like: "She was so progressive, she was regressive," but they might've said something else, too.

Then our story continues in proper form...

"Us freaks must stick together," said the demon to the saint.

The skyline was beautiful on fire, and he watched in awe of the hues and was dazed by its many perforated saturations.

A critical moment came for him when he pondered the nature of birth and wondered whether everything, given enough time, could eventually grow back—if not over, an ever-changing landscape in perpetual flux. And he thought that that was a beautiful thought. The end of exits, or the constant flow of corridors.

Duane was getting tired and decided to transfigure himself into a couch and spend his remaining days lounging about and taking in all the brouhaha of the inanimate life. He kept up his strength by eating stray cats which the lovely (now middle-aged) nurse fed him—his cushions acting like a Venus flytrap of sorts. The years passed, and Duane was eventually killed in a house fire started by a mad arsonist. An inscription on a surviving cushion read:

Treacherous beauty is a blinding bolt.

—the hairpin harpy

And who lit the fire, you might ask? Dogman, of course, and when they asked him why he'd done it, cleansed the earth of this grotesque and audacious evil, and how he knew that Duane—the all-powerful and elusive demon—was hiding in the upholstery of a high-end sofa, he replied, "Following my limbs, following my whims."

Thus spake Dogman.

Chapter 21: Code Unknown #2

John had a talent for self-destruction.

George believed that superstition and blind ignorance led the world.

Joyce loved him with full abandon precisely because he didn't deserve it.

Richard allowed his dreams to live undisturbed. To linger in his mind unthreatened by the sting of realization.

Gwen believed that everyone was eventually disappointing.

Cocaine rattled through Joyce's brain and became the impetus for a great doomsday discovery.

Richard was sincere in his intention to be kind to others, although he often went about it in as crude a way as possible.

George's wish for solitude was thwarted by his lack of money and distaste for the outdoors.

Joyce believed that sex was the only reason to go on living and not a very good one at that.

John thought the truth wasn't worth it.

Gwen looked at popular culture as the low-dosage variety.

A hobbyist's choosing. A three-star retreat. She needed something stronger, something to really dull the pain.

George asked the writer what he was composing. The writer responded with a vowel, a pause, and two syllables.

Richard thought that without selfishness to anchor love, you lose its humanity, as humanity itself is a selfish enterprise.

As John recounted his childhood, he realized he was an unreliable narrator.

George stepped left, then dodged right, shards of shit peppered the sidewalk. Biological shrapnel from some unholy beast. Large and looming. This was the type born of kings.

Richard referred to her as a "beautiful love receptacle." Even in close company, Richard spoke in code.

John could see the top of his brother's head shine through in interlaced rays. He was happy he outranked his brother in both age and hair density.

Gwen believed that beauty was found in the nuance and arrangement of ordinary symbols. A harmonizing and clashing of tones paired just so. A serving of rocket fuel in the guise of fruit punch.

John despised convictions, although he himself held many and none so obviously contradictory than his conviction regarding the stupidity and absurdity of all convictions.

John was horrified and humiliated when he realized that the entire point of the game was not to call attention to its asinine nature. His once-playful ruminations had become pointed interrogations of such a ferocious magnitude that even his most adored and ardent layers crumbled under the weight of his scrutiny. A merciless extermination was underway. Nothing could be done. The machine was in motion.

He mowed the lawn under the dimming sun and ingested a couple of mushrooms he saw along the edge of his yard. Soon the night sky was brimming with delights, and the hallucinogenic effects of his backyard pilgrimage were well underway.

He saw an eye in the sky and wondered, "Who the hell was up there?"

Electrical outlets were one of the many viewpoints from which God viewed the universe.

"And quite simply, it was a case of bad manners," said the broken puppet with inverted eyes, and when they asked him if he could see his heart, he scoffed and responded: "It's pitch-black in here!"

In the end, it was the sanctity of the ridiculous and the malleability of the absurd that saved them and restored their dignity and maybe even their faith.

A born patriot in the eyes of the law.

The prisoner's view of a cracked cement wall did not excite him. But after *many* hours of staring at this collage of meaninglessness, he began to see it differently. At first, noticing only its indentations and grooves, which took on an air of abstraction, which then transformed and took on familiar and visible forms, which then developed into a complicated labyrinthine narrative, which then evolved and enriched itself with each subsequent viewing. All of which happened without any effort on his part. Simply looking and waiting were enough to bring this masterpiece into the light.

Another portal of abstraction appears to John in the innards of a traffic drum.

The defeat of Sir Ludwig by the brash Sir Winslow was bloody and brutal—words unfit to describe the joy, exhilaration, defeat, momentary nihilism, shame, and self-pity associated with the act.

A montage of everything we've seen up to date.

It was only later in life that June realized how good it would feel to be forgotten. All your sins and triumphs and failures and defeats gone. To reenter nothingness as if you'd never left.

After exiting the theater, he realized that the film's subtext had spoken something along the lines of, "We are small, and we are brief. Do not presume we can understand it all."

Over the course of Dorothy's battle with her archnemesis, she became more and more like her, in the end, resembling her entirely.

Joan attempted to give a shit, but sometimes it was just too hard.

He dreams of drug-addled superheroes. She dreams of octopi in Berlin.

She stretched out in the park and gazed around at the open space before an oddball neighbor came over, complaining about her recent injury, stating that when she'd broken her ribs, she had—for the first time ever—realized the fragility of her meat pod.

A symbolic image from a Tuesday night dream?

A balloon is lost,
A coin is tossed,
And man's fate?
Arbitrary and
Innate.

A discussion between symbols forecasted in the minds of the participants who are really at the mercy of something else entirely.

Bradley was fascinated by life's basic mystery: now you see it, now you don't.

She rode her strangeness to new heights and lonely depths. And yet she wasn't lonely—or wasn't lonely in the way most people think of lonely. She was tired and bored and sometimes would mistakenly assume another person was the answer to this conundrum, but that wasn't true, and each time she tried to solve the problem this way, it always ended badly, and usually with tears, and mostly from them.

Dreams with a pale horse were often foreboding in one sense or another.

The private eye known as Chuck is fascinated by the rudimentary mystery of how one thing becomes another—not to mention the complex means of recycling that the universe has devised for itself on the grandest and most microscopic of scales. All the cases he has ever dealt with are, in one way or another, based on this fundamental and baffling mystery of consumption, transformation, and regurgitation.

Sipping a milkshake and waiting for Rick to return from the bathroom, Anne hallucinates a wave of color and wonders if it's all just som

Forced to   d finishes
his cigare   t death;
his goddam   h ways
and cur   er than
having   . "Die,
strange   nto the
abys   ds the
pave

Wh   films
he lik   of an
exp   sual
eleme   for
him,   radic
laugh   elief
valv   ension
once

Th   riced 6
lamb   o grow—
and th   o avail.

The   highway,
and it o   with the
inconvenience

And the satyrs danced and praised their queen, but she did not like the frivolous nature of their tune.

When the soldiers asked him if he thought war was the devil's business, he said he thought that the question was a silly one and that the devil didn't exist—at least not in the way that they thought of him—and that he was just another facet of God, but God after He'd ingested something or smoked something... something like synthetic cathinones, which altered Him, and could make Him excited and horny and paranoid and delirious and violent with genocidal urges.

The broadcast was rudely interrupted by a competing signal that made the onscreen images blur and twist and compete for the light of center stage.

The TV made up his mind and chose his inevitable course.

Stupidity is stronger than steel, and intelligence has its roots in nihilism—thus spake the asshole.

And the lava flowed, and destruction was upon them, and man no longer cared about its trivial pursuits; destruction provided clarity, and its genius was short-lived.

"The world is made up of signs, symbols, and tones—nothing more," thought Judd Quinn.

Signs tell us things, and symbols represent things, and tones infuse things, and time changes things.

You will go to bed a liberal and wake up a fascist; God's a real joker; He wrote the genius of the masses.

Joan believed that, in the jungle, everyone gets everything they want... eventually, or in filth, it will be found.

Achilles has yet to reach that fucking tortoise.

The artist is best described as the spokesman for the spirit of his or her age, tied to it, and usually beaten and bested by it; his or her art is nothing if not a response to it and, oftentimes, an attack against it.

Old pirated gems on ancient VHS technology.

Stepping through the portal, he realized that he was in yet another maze, but better this one than that one, he thought.

Even though they are all the same, the change comes from the name.

He laughed for no better reason than he could.

After she spoke to him, he said, "Your sentence is a riddle that I will not even bother to decipher."

The wolf panted as it stared at the hare and envisioned its corpse between its rotten and vicious teeth.

Two junkies attack a vegan in a dirty corridor.

The sisters were out on the rocky terrain seeking out lone wanderers to discuss theological questions with, like, "If God decided to go back to the beginning of time, would He even be aware of having made the leap? Or would His mind or His consciousness—or whatever we imagine His thought process is like—be the same at the beginning as it is now? Or when He leaps in time, does He go back into His former self with no knowledge of His future self? Is God able to see all of time all the time? Is God's sense of time so abstract and foreign that no conjuring of words can even approach its magnificence? Why do mortals ask such questions if they can never know anything definite relating to the mind of God?" Most wanderers paid them no mind, and the sisters eventually stumbled on, lost in thoughts of their own making, in a westward direction.

And some said that philosophizing was a form of cowardice and that the world was sedated with feelings.

And when he finally went crazy, it was because he realized that he was right.

And then he laughed...

Chapter 22: Modern Lovers

PART 1

He had a sniper rifle and some claymore mines, and he knew that at times like these you stayed down and played dumb.

He hoped he'd be able to slap his balls against her backside (or *derrière*) at some later point.

Master of resignation, he knew when to pick a fight.

Not far from their bunker, carved in a tree, "Romantic suggestions from moving molecules," signed, "Master of War."

In one day, he killed 6 Germans and captured two enemy foxholes and was given an extra ration of chow for his fortunate, albeit formulaic, efforts.

She watched a lot of cartoons and courtroom dramas and a few choice reruns of classic sitcoms.

She wanted to be Sweden—or was it Switzerland?

And she knew that all great works could be easily misinterpreted.

She was the personification of wolf-like tenacity, and she

was offended by the randomness of his weak and insensitive nose. The way he forced his schnoz upon all egregious odors, without etiquette or ethic, and always spoke superfluously of the examined scent—an olfactory dilettante.

Icarus of odors, humdrum desert by your side, sickness and perversion east, abide the sounds and vibrations of the westward tide.

He displayed great poise under duress and was seen as the star athlete at St. John's Elementary School. A pursuer of ecstatic truths and wild rebounds.

He was insensitive to uncertainties.

He decided to descend to its depths, thinking that at least he'd have his dignity, when, in fact, it was the first thing to go, and for all his assumptions and premeditation, it appeared to be a bottomless fucking pit.

She stepped into the belly of her shadow, and when someone asked her about religion, she spoke of her love for storytelling.

Could I... should I... would I...

And just because of the fool she was, she decided to draw a bit from heaven and a lot from hell.

Upon drinking too much whiskey, he was visited by the demon Mush-Mush. His cock was plunged into deep and irrevocable relaxation, a sleeping beauty whose slumber did not stir no matter who kissed it.

For him, the world was a jumbled-up game of telephone. Lines crossed and syllables mispronounced. And he sometimes wondered if there was a direct connection between certainty and idiocy.

When the judge asked why she'd smashed the glass into poor Donny's face, she said she was trying to give expression to his inner monstrosity.

Just by working there, she became part of a secret club she didn't know she wanted to be part of.

"A part-time travesty." That's what the pedestrian said when referencing the omnibus of his rambling thoughts.

In the belly of the machine, one of the workers referenced her with a disparaging remark, commenting on the color of her skin and mixing unusual inflection with negative connotations and a harsh grimace to boot. He sneered at her, casting the spell and seeing its outcome. She walked away. One week later, while he was occupying himself with a piss, she knocked him out and laid his face in the urinal. She took multiple photos and sent them around the office with colorful captions, casting the violent demise of his character and the swift end of her corporate career.

It was hard for them to understand the reasoning behind his disgust. Everyone else seemed to be enjoying it, but its taste and temperature were revolting, and with each mouthful, he felt his gag reflex kick harder, ramping up to full swing, sending him into volatile spasms as he tried his best to politely swallow each tepid mouthful. They couldn't understand the symptoms he seemed to be displaying and, therefore, could administer no cure. They wrote him off as an eccentric and callous fool, unaware of the visceral rebellion taking place in the man's innards.

And like any good artists, they were natural-born killers.

PART 2

They met in late autumn in the Year of the Pig.

The night before, she dreamt of palm trees and Piccadilly Circus.

They started small, environmental waste, and she enjoyed the thought of an indirect killing. A plastic cap swallowed by an orphan aardvark, tossed haphazardly years before, lying in wait to choke the little son of a gun. A series of indiscriminate murders by asphyxiation or malnutrition.

They headed west in an old Buick and took Highway 42 down an old turnpike. They stopped off at a gas station for supplies, and it was in this instant that they graduated from typical road-tripping citizens to marauder and outlaw. Terms she would turn over in her brain in the coming days, applying layers of definitions to the newly acquired identity she and her sweetheart had garnered; a title tied and wrapped to their faces, lampooned and fictionalized by the media, killed and reconstructed by the public, a resurrection in the modern era. But she wondered if she stripped her name and hid her identity whether the deeds themselves still persisted, haunting her, even under the alias of Linda or Suzanne with dyed red hair and an eyebrow ring. Could she slide easily into a new identity? Maybe working at a dry cleaner's—Linda with red hair—and daily, minute by minute, little by little, she would begin to assume and assimilate into this new role, then would the killings and robberies of her past cease to be in the fabric of time, her time, if no one remembered them, because no one brought them up, because she was someone else—Linda with red hair—or because the victims, all of them, were dead or forgotten or because they too forgot or moved on? Were ghosts only plausible when the fiction was fresh? Tied to the retelling, or perhaps they transformed and acted like a succubus or incubus nestled in the unconscious, using dreams as a sexualized vehicle to cultivate and prolong their imprint—a procreating dream—bearing demon offspring, pure unconscious subterfuge; spawns of a real-life crime actualizing under layers of strangely contextualized subtext in order to continue to exist under a new mnemonic guise. Linda with red hair. She was brought back to the present moment when she heard a shout. She turned and saw him fire his snub-nosed revolver at an overly vocal onlooker who took the bullet square in the face and slumped to the ground with a gaping hole for a forehead. He yelled at her to hurry, referring to his pistol as a blunderbuss, which made her remember that he referred to his penis as his pistol, distinctions that she found a bit odd but learned to live with, as they now shared a fate tied by bloodshed and a common narrative thread.

The news never pictured them alone, always together, and because they couldn't find any photos of them actually together, they photoshopped them or used a diagonal line to artificially splice their pictures together. She thought of this media-driven coupling as a form of marriage, a bond that she couldn't or wouldn't break, stronger than any religious union, and more binding than any lawful documentation.

Her musical taste remained current with modern trends and was therefore on the cutting edge of mediocrity. This being the very reason why they killed her.

And she craved an inverse enlightenment, a transcendent leap backwards.

Knowing that no one could ever be truly understood, she hoped for a favorable misunderstanding.

He made up for his well-behaved youth by stirring up a plague worthy of the Middle Ages during his adulthood.

He was supposedly anti-fascist and pro-censorship. A dichotomy warranting doom, and our hero—tommy gun in hand—unloaded the bulk of his clip, sending mixed-meat confetti at the adjacent white wall and rendering his foe obsolete and pulpy.

And on their wedding day, he kept singing, "Her and me and the devil makes three."

The trouble began when he realized that art, or the peak, or the zenith of some somnambulant adventure, could only be attained by the individual, while the collective could only offer a lesser but palatable consensus. Ease of consumption being the key turn of phrase for all menial-type creations which all suffered for their collective adherence to an assured and pleasant agreement over the intense and personalized mania of one solitary and delusional source.

He sometimes performed feats of celestial magic, a dime-store conjuror of ephemeral tricks.

It was there to be interpreted however they chose, as myth or fact, right or wrong; a chameleon molded to the whims and fancy of the observer, ready to adhere to their judgment without complaint or compromise.

And he also knew that a grand illusion was the cornerstone and kernel necessary to survive the treacherous tide and ubiquitous disaster calling itself "Life." And when the peach was eaten and only the pit remained, few options were available.

In utter disarray, he decided to end the game and hang himself from the rafters. He was sick and tired of the looting and killing and fucking and scheming and charming and the delirium and the boredom and the weirdness of the profane and the sanctity of the chaos and all the order of an organized workweek. He was done with it all and only hoped for the barrenness of an empty and nonexistent future. The holy grail residing somewhere within the dark and incorruptible void.

But before he could end it, he knew he needed to provide a proper farewell, love of his life in tow, and he thought that maybe a solitary suicide was not a befitting exit for a soul as carnivorous and rapturous as his own. He talked with his sweetheart and set up a final score. One whose survival rate neared zero, and when he thought about it, it sent butterflies fluttering from his guts in anticipation of his grand and righteous finale.

A grand total of 1,024 bullets were discharged during the final hurrah, resulting in 27 dead and an estimated total by today's standards of $325,000 worth of damage and $700,000 worth of cash stolen from the virtuous banking establishment. He went in alone, not wishing for any harm to come to his love, knowing the grim odds of survival, leaving her outside in the getaway car. Although by some macabre twist of fate, he had miraculously succeeded in dodging all incoming blows while acquiring the loot and administering a substantial amount of carnage to those standing in his way. A single, solitary bullet fired by a rookie cop—the lone shot fired during their getaway—landed square in the back of her head, splattering her brains onto the windshield and resulting in the car swerving violently from side to side before he could take control and maneuver it to safety and out onto the open desert roads.

PART 3

In the days following her death, he was stuck between moments of crippling sadness, precipitated by awful bouts of weeping, and incorrigible horniness. Each night he seemed to grasp the hand of some maiden, young or old, ugly or beautiful, and in a heated and exhilarated passion, make love or fuck them until dawn or oblivion or whichever would come first. Exhaustion greeted him favorably at the end of these sexual sessions, but within an hour of the lady's departure, the hurt and pain returned, thumping around in excruciating agony, growing more dense and perverse with each passing minute until a raging hard-on and a psychosexual legacy came to his rescue, resulting in debilitating masturbation sessions in the afternoon and a return to the bar in the evenings to woo some passing flame for his nightly escapades.

She, on the other hand, woke up groggy and drunk from what seemed to have been a long trip south. The decorative style consisted mostly of dark and vibrant reds as if the color spectrum had been radically reduced to adhere to a strict and rudimentary regime. The room was quaint but cozy and had all the necessary bedroom accoutrements, but before inventory could be taken, the door edged open, and a horned figure crept forward. He spoke evenly and with a gentleman's verve.

"Good day, my name's Bartleby."

He gave her a tour of hell, which began at a warehouse-like grocery store with aisles that were extremely narrow and incredibly dense; items were packed 100 feet high in a labyrinth of numberless rows. Bartleby was a kind and permitting guide, offering her the opportunity to explore as her whims took hold; she gallivanted down the frozen-food section and met a couple of other hellish occupants who nodded politely as they shimmied by. There weren't many other shoppers, and at various points, she came across open sections, which resembled living rooms and reminded her of a furniture outlet she once visited when she was a little girl. In one room, she found a dollhouse that looked a lot like the one she used to have as a kid. She noticed that none of the items had any price tags, and when she quizzed her host about this fact, he replied that everything was free, at least for the moment.

Meanwhile, he, the horny mourner, set out in search of the proper opioid to reestablish equilibrium among his days. The pandemonium his life had become at the loss of his love and the violent ricocheting between grief and sexual gratification was proving to be the very heart of madness. He needed a solution to lull his fits, and he needed it now. In a destitute state, he hit the road, walking aimlessly, praying to the gods for some sign or solace until an illuminated ad on the side of an old bus station caught his eye. Pure coincidence? Divine intervention? Who could tell? But the outcome quite literally catapulted him into the cosmos. The ad spoke of an immediate departure, leaving Sunday, funded by an internet billionaire, seeking brave pioneers for an off-world colonizing project on the beautiful, dust-covered planet Mars.

As the days or months or years passed by (it was difficult to distinguish time in hell), she noticed an increasing decrepitude accumulating over everything like a fine dust—hell was losing its initial luster. She noticed that even Bartleby, her once kind and gracious host, was falling into disrepair both physically and emotionally. His words were harder to decipher; he mumbled often, and sometimes he simply growled. His head had also shifted, sinking lower towards his abdomen, and one day, she noticed his head was now located on his sternum, and 3 tentacles had sprouted from the top of his neck. She didn't immediately ask about the changes, as she was a new occupant and didn't want to offend, but one day, gathering courage, she asked him, and his speech was hard to grasp but certain chosen terms rang out in her ears like "subjective catacombs" and "cumulative trip downward" and "degenerate debauchee."

Hell was becoming a drab affair, and she pined for the good ol' days with her love—the canoodling and drive-thru dinners—she wondered to what extent hell's creativity could continue on its downward trajectory, entropy *à la max*. The giant walls of provisions had long ago rotted, and the modern and high-fashion common areas were overgrown with reddish ooze and slithering flora. Yet she acquiesced day by day, and in some deranged excitement, she actually looked forward to the new progressions downward. What new monstrosity could hell acquire to captivate her imagination? Then, one day, out of the blue, Bartleby edged into her room, and just as if a magic spell had been cast, her room, with its cirrhosis-like aesthetic, returned to its initial glory. As he spoke his words of introduction, with perfect articulation, she was overcome by grogginess and déjà vu and a strange sensation at having just woken from a long trip.

On the rocket heading to Mars, he thought about his past life and what the future had in store, and he looked out the circular window of the spacecraft and watched Earth exit the frame, and he wondered if life was as simple as that: what was in the frame, and what was out of it. He tossed this query about in his brain as the dark side of the moon passed before the window and, therefore, in front of his eyes.

And when he died, he saw an immense blue curtain, and it shifted with reckless abandon.

Chapter 23: Holly

There seemed to be a guiding force underneath, an indifferent watchmaker guiding the labyrinth of the cosmos, issuing directions with amoral intent, infinitely complex and divisive, with each moment cast being a testament to this immortal and terrible intelligence. An artful stroke of magic, frightful and beautiful, a multitude of contradictions in flux and developed God knows where by some madman or other—a good God or an evil dog—the deity does not deign to show its design (or its presence, which may or may not be hiding in plain sight).

Holly pondered this and that and thought back to a man who'd explained that the world was simply governed by ignorance and superstition, politicians and conspiracies, a thin layer of order sculpted by man in a hostile and chaotic universe, and she thought about how this made her feel, its simplicity, but also its arrogance and assumptions. The pride and hubris to assume that we make our own decisions at all, that we exist beyond the mere puppetry of a blind and unyielding will, that our perceptions can be trusted, hierarchies believed, that we are not simply roller coasters welded to the tracks, that choice, even in the realm of chaos, is possible and change and bliss even a remote possibility.

But then again, maybe that's the way it is, or maybe it's a tapestry of half-truths woven together from a collection of hundreds or thousands of cut-up beliefs and obnoxious certainties. Or maybe each individual's perspective is an adjoining piece of an incomprehensible puzzle, a multi-faceted riddle with infinite possible solutions. Puppets and masters moving alongside one another, shedding beliefs and roles and purposes to reveal contradictory desires and hidden agendas; an absurd journey guided by dreams and choices or wills and fate, each proposed narrative and perspective as insane and ordinary as the next. Relative states of verbal mischief governing the heads of an army of delusional and earnest apes, or a sea of detectives rationalizing the great mystery of the divine, or an antithetical order so baffling and longstanding that each lifetime will never even glimpse one one-millionth of its overarching scheme. Or perhaps each day is simply a repetition of one single everlasting day, with all prior days being but a memory in the mind of the dreamer; permutations and exaggerations are all part of the great puzzle—the infinite, vile, beautiful, insane, gorgeous, and horrific divide we have characterized and crunched down and given the symbol we articulate as life.

Holly was exhausted by this train of thought and cursed that cocksucker George for having begun it with an earlier fatuous remark about a president he disliked. Him sitting opposite her in a well-lit diner as the howling winter winds bellowed outside. She cut a piece of her friend's octopus and savored the sapid meat, cozy and content in the posh trappings of her favorite eatery.

(Holly's dream: part 1)

Tentacle expanding in infinite divisions, the madman turns sane, and the sane goes mad, two sides of the same coin.

That night she dreamt of many strange things: communes in the woods, piano teachers, predators...

And Sisyphus and the rolling rocks sang the cocksucker blues.

Song verse (cocksucker blues):

Was I born in Sodom or south of Gomorrah?

Is my body rotten or just my aura?

Renewal of creation and destruction (continuous cycles)

If language is a virus...

Repeat chorus

God's coin seen from Joyce's perspective, or the cocooned contradiction.

(Zahir) looks like this --------------- on the transverse plane.

And Gwen dreamt she was a worm with wings.

And then she told Lenny about being in the belly of some beast, and he asked her what happened next, and she replied, "And then I woke up."

"And where were you?"

"With you, across from an old man and a kid, at a diner, floating on a little rock, drifting through space."

"Does everything always repeat?"

"NOTHING IS TRUE AND EVERYTHING IS PERMITTED… and mostly with slight variations. At least that's what the tiger told me at the end of the lane."

"How'd he look?"

"Goddamn infinite."

And then she looked up at the ceiling and noticed its decor, admiring its frightful parallel cuts and deep incisors. Bloody hell, she thought.

And at that, a west wind howled, and they admired the architectural symmetry in the jaws of their predicament.

As the old man sat bare-assed on the restaurant shitter admiring his artwork, he thought of the sanctity of the ridiculousness, the joys of the absurd, and the beauty and perfection of an absolute and bottomless sense of nothingness. Life has its charms, he thought, and then he imagined a golden astrolabe as he pinched off a beefy loaf in the mouth of the bowl below.

Chapter 24: Lenny, or: Out-Monster the Monster

The artist tries to be a poet, and the poet tries to be a prankster, and the prankster tries to be a god.

But one only becomes a god reluctantly.

He knew he'd probably die laughing in the face of some schmuck, a sinister rebuttal to their delusional and hilarious megalomania, which he also seemed to be suffering from—his taking the less serious form cultivated alongside a healthy dose of failure and apathy, nullifying most conceivable routes which ambition and ignorance would have thereby flung him down, resulting in less time lost. But more time for what exactly? Indirect detours with benign odysseys?

The killer would see the insult hiding behind Lenny's eyes, and Lenny would not be able to contain the laughter choked behind his grin. The ensuing outburst ravishing the murderer's psyche, laying siege (as nothing else had) to the walls of their identity, crashing down in one fell swoop. Rage and fury unknown to the killer until now, spurred on by an animalistic vulnerability, would pour forth as he stared into Lenny's bright and joyous eyes. Lenny would smile and enjoy his last hurrah as the demented creature crushed his fucking head in with whatever blunt object lay close at hand. But then Lenny remembered that he was a god and death was a foreign matter; a mystery he couldn't conceive beyond fictional incarnations conducted Saturday mornings as mental musings for his lonely and loopy mind.

His brain was a balancing act, and the ball could roll to either side of crazy.

Lenny was sick of being cast as the poor, pathetic loser and decided that a change of image was in order. He put on his posh, expensive threads and went out into the world with the same "fuck it" attitude that had folded itself onto itself endless times before; his founding principle transformed into an infinite and complex spiritual origami, rebranded and repositioned with each costume change. The kernel of a simple idea with a multitude of variants, shifting the "fuck it" mentality in whichever direction Lenny happened to want to maneuver, from dismissing an event outright to joining in with reckless and gleeful abandon; all decisions passed the subtle tonal filter accompanying those two beautiful syllables.

Trying to do the duties of a god with the weaknesses of a man.

Unsure what to say and not wanting to be a complete piece of shit, Lenny congratulated him on having an opinion.

As Lenny thought about the world, he thought about how many snouts and cocks and ears and assholes there were and how few hearts. This never failed to make him sad, and he sometimes thought about having one bad day... over and over again.

He wondered from time to time if he shouldn't end the world, sick as he was of it—playing the fool, the heartthrob, the celebrity, the deviant, the saint, and the demon, and sometimes all in a single day. Lenny was often tired, and when bouts of tiredness lingered on too long, his sadistic side took the forefront, and he'd usually end up devouring some unlucky soul as nourishment to refill his half-empty cup. Hunger being the basis for most sins.

Lenny sometimes joked that when he finally met God, the Big One—the one with a capital *G*—he'd kick Him right in His ass. He said it'd be easy because His asshole was everywhere and its circumference unknown.

Lenny was walking with his roommate, June, a Black transsexual with a shaved head, C-cup breasts, and a seven-and-a-half-inch penis. They were rudely interrupted by a sermonizing woman expelling inane grad-school rhetoric who abruptly demonized Lenny the Wolf God, while praising June, for no other reason than to confirm her own ridiculous bias. Lenny was annoyed, but June—beautiful creature that she was—was irate for once again being bothered and expected to conform to yet another worldview that wasn't her own. She camouflaged her feelings well and invited the grad student over for dinner that night, apologizing in advance for Lenny's atrocious rudeness and outright stupidity. When the grad student arrived and entered their apartment, June struck her in the face with an axe, and Lenny fed her into a meat grinder, and they ate her, cunt and all. And when Lenny asked June if that was her *new* cat in the corner, she replied, "Yes, that's my pussy."

But then he thought that maybe there might have been a better way to deal with the situation, but time was a fickle mistress, and she'd already moved on.

After drinking two bottles of Bordeaux, June drunkenly exclaimed that she was Geneva, the god of destruction, and they sang the "Higgs Boson Blues."

Lenny belonged to Orpheus' bloodline.

He once read that words are symbols that posit shared memories. It was one of the most beautiful sequences he'd come across, a simple articulation of a complex system. And Lenny held Borges in very high esteem.

"Good and evil are part-time occupations in most people's hearts."

Lenny often noted that in order to do something beautiful, one often had to bury something very ugly in one's soul. Them's the breaks, he thought. Batman needs his Joker. And Joker needs his Gunnery Sergeant Hartman. And Gunnery Sergeant Hartman needs his POV.

***

While watching a movie on a cold winter night, Lenny's phone rings right at the exact moment when the female protagonist yells, "Die, you not-see scum!" and fires a shotgun at her enemy's head—which explodes—just as he pauses the TV set.

After a short and uneventful call, he focuses his attention back on the TV and notices the pattern of gristle and blood up on the screen. It looks suspiciously like a swastika, and Lenny wonders if this was a purposeful act on the part of the filmmakers, or perhaps it was a serendipitous moment of accidental creativity, developed by some unconscious urge on the part of the moviemaking team. If he were to make a movie, he too would inject it with subliminal imagery, like single frames of explicit content dispersed in fractal patterns across a 2-hour runtime, or an image of a limbless and headless horse falling smack in the middle of some CGI family film, right at the precipice when some big cathartic emotional payoff was about to ensue.

***

A long time ago, hundreds of years in fact, Lenny donned the attire of a sleuth or, as some might say, a detective. Back in those days, mysteries required less technological savvy to solve and instead required a more robust and fascist tint. Pain and torture were often rewarded with vital information when the right individual was subjected to it, and Lenny was rather good at picking the proper canaries to make sing. He rarely felt bad about the pain and violence he inflicted, but hundreds of years later, when he looked back on those times, he was always a little embarrassed. Regret rarely entered into the equation, but he couldn't help but think that there must have been a better and easier way of reconciling the information he needed with the actions he was forced to undertake. More modern methods revolved around blackmail and targeted attacks on someone's public image or persona, with or without suitable evidence, of course. The modern world had weaponized the rumor, and its ability to wreak havoc was equivalent to a spiritual nuke bomb. As information was exceedingly quick to disperse from one outlet to the next, a man, woman, or child's reputation could be vanquished within a 5-minute window if conditions were properly primed.

Lenny woke up to the radio broadcasting the morning news, subjecting his newly awakened mind to cringe-inducing matters of vile and idiotic opinion. Today it told him about an old holiday film that was being targeted by a lamebrain posse of dullards and nitwits who thought the climax's payoff didn't justify the narrative's arc. The disconnect between these people's sheltered reality and their righteous need to push their pompous and ignorant tastes—all the while censoring the world's content—was condescending, infantile, and totalitarian. How come they couldn't just turn the fucking thing off like a regular person if they didn't like it? But then Lenny knew that "these people" were not out to make the world a better place; they had achieved their position in life (most of which were of modest standing) in the same way that they had decided to deal with this celebrated Christmas movie, by bitching about it until they got their way like psychotic, annoying, and cunty kids. They used bitching as a means of exerting power, and Lenny really fucking hated them today. He didn't know why, on this particular morning, he was so revved up by this. Perhaps it had something to do with *it* being the first signal to have entered his wolfish brain so early in the morning. Either way, he decided to call the radio station and voice his support and try and gather a few names from the roster championing this ridiculous bid. He got a few names and found out that two of them were in fact married. He decided that they should pay the price for this abysmal moral degradation society was once again succumbing to. He thought of the whole rigmarole as similar to the book burnings he'd witnessed at the hands of another bunch of cunts—those Nazi fucks who burned or degraded works of art they didn't like or agree with, although, to be fair, these modern assholes operated in a much tamer and kinder fashion. He waited until Christmas Eve to deploy his plan and sharpened his teeth in anticipation.

When Lenny got to their house on Christmas Eve and they opened the door, he was instantly annoyed to find that they had two children and were, in fact, not terrible people—annoying, yes, but certainly not evil. They reminded him of the ass-kissers in grade school who ratted out their peers but were, all in all, good students. He decided that killing them and eating them was not the manner in which to deal with this situation. But ol' Lenny had some devious tricks up his godlike sleeves, and he asked them if they'd like to hear a wonderful Christmas tale. The kids cheered, and the parents smiled, and Lenny clacked his tongue, and just like that, the walls dissolved, and the whole lot of them found themselves in a new environment filled with snow and reindeer and elves and all the accoutrements of a holiday special; in other words, Lenny had transported them into the animated land of their much-hated holiday film.

But his plan backfired, and Lenny, who anticipated this adventure playing out like some cruel and unorthodox nightmare, was once again disappointed. The fault in his plan stemmed from his aesthetic philosophy. Lenny—the purist, particularly when it came to the construction and induction of visions—liked to stray from the sensational and create his worlds as authentically as he could; thus, no horrible monsters from other dimensions or films or books would cross over, and the characters represented here were all faithful adaptations of the televised version. The kids were having a great time and hugged and thanked Lenny; and the parents, a little disturbed by the sudden change of scenery, were nonetheless satisfied and cheerful once they found their footing and noticed the smiles on their kids' faces. Lenny was getting frustrated and decided to try a different approach with his plan.

Lenny extended the timeline and forced the family to stay in this senseless place for a whole month. He, too, would stay, witnessing the boredom and annoyance the family would surely feel at having to be stuck in this overly bright and happy make-believe world.

He told them that he'd accidentally set the timer wrong using lingo directly lifted from an '80s time-traveling trilogy as a means of explanation. The family was worried, but Lenny assured them that there was nothing to worry about and that time *here* did not correspond to actual time, and at the end of the month, when they'd all returned to the comfort of their living room, no more than 30 minutes would have elapsed in the modern, everyday world. Stern glares from the matriarch of the family told Lenny that he'd done well.

The month went on as expected, slowly the family was becoming increasingly agitated and fed up with the overly happy elves and the kind reindeer, their one-dimensional personas irritating to the nth degree. One of the children, the boy, smashed the head off an old snowman that kept bothering him with remarks about the weather, and the young girl bit a reindeer that kept snuggling up against her, and the parents each stopped talking to one another and spent most of their time alone on opposing ends of the map which consisted of only a few small acres. Lenny began to feel bad too but stuck to his timeline; only a fortnight left, he thought. But as time marched on, he changed his mind and decided, in the goodness of the holiday spirit, to reconcile the family and break a few of his own rules in order to bring about a cathartic and beautiful denouement to this strange and horrible holiday adventure.

One morning, Lenny gathered the family and told them he had a special prize for them, a surprise gift. The family was in no mood for such frivolous festivities but went along with the trope as there wasn't much else to do. Once the clan was gathered, he lifted the tarp to reveal their prize, and underneath were 4 shining flamethrowers, one for each of them. Renewed happiness and smiles adorned the faces of the entire group, and the young boy kissed Lenny's hand, and the mother praised his evil soul.

They went to work almost immediately and fried those cocksuckers; reindeer and elves were being torched, and Santa was being dismembered, and the whole scene reeked of burnt sugar. The paterfamilias was displaying a real talent for destruction, and even his wife couldn't help but notice. Lenny smiled at the new developments and helped the kids finish off the last of those bastard elves with sharpened candy canes and a 9-inch bowie knife. And when they finished killing those overly congenial minions, they noticed loud, rhythmic yells coming from behind a large snowbank, and Lenny knew what these sounds represented, and he decided to shield the kids from the horror of the scene, and he took them to the other end of the small made-up world, while the kids' parents fucked each other's brains out in the freshly fallen snow.

They returned home soon after the carnage ended, and Lenny made up some harebrained excuse as to why he was able to expedite their departure. When they arrived back in the living room, only 15 minutes had elapsed according to the clock on the wall. The family thanked Lenny for their adventure, although they seemed a bit shocked and embarrassed now that they'd returned to the comfort of their formerly well-adjusted skins. Lenny wished them a merry Christmas and left without further ado.

Outside, the family's cat hissed at him, and he ate the little fucker in one quick bite.

When he got to the bar, the man next to him asked, "How does one begin a story? A difficult question for any author who wishes to impart their tale with aplomb and gravitas, lending weight and dexterity to the telling and allowing it to sink and absorb at the proper subterranean depths." Lenny told him just to start talking and quit exactly when he'd achieved that perfect, fragile height, the one at the top of the circle, right before the drop-off, just before the beginning of another loop. Stop there, and you've created a masterwork. Stop there, and you've achieved something remarkable. "And don't forget," he added, "the end looks a lot like the beginning."

Twenty-five years or so before, Lenny was confronted by another god named George. Although there weren't many gods living on Earth—they numbered around the low fifties (more than most would have assumed, I guess)—they were nonetheless rather antagonistic to one another. Lenny never really knew why this was but suspected vanity and pride; the gods were not used to being on equal footing with those around them, presumably threatened by the presence of another powerful figure. Anyway, George, who was a rather annoying god, irritable and loud, had encountered Lenny by happenchance at the local supermarket, and Lenny—prankster extraordinaire—had cast a spell on George, forcing his eyeballs to come loose every time he heard his name called. Lenny wasn't even sure why he'd decided to do this and forgot about it almost as fast as he'd cast it. George, on the other hand, ended up losing both his eyes to the prank, and even though he could regenerate his lost hardware, the process was lengthy and incredibly painful. When George found out that it was Lenny who'd cursed him (he found out because drunken Lenny had bragged about it to Bruce when Bruce had told him that he'd seen George (and George had told him about his eyes and his trouble), who in turn told Linda, who shuttled the gossip to Julie, who was currently sleeping with Brad, who ended up being George's neighbor), he decided to kill Lenny once and for all.

There was only one place in the whole world where a god could die. It was on Easter Island in the southeastern Pacific Ocean. How the gods knew that this was the only place was subject to rumor and speculation. Presumably, one of the gods from antiquity had accidentally wounded or maimed themselves there, and through sheer chance, they'd discovered one of the spots, if not the only one, where a god's invincibility was suspended. Over the years, some gods, sick of the immortal way of life, had gone to Easter Island to commit suicide and put an end to the game once and for all. George challenged Lenny to a duel there, and each god was given a 9mm pistol, and in an open field, about 100 yards apart, they yelled, "*Go!*" and began firing haphazardly at one another like some old Wild West showdown. Lenny was wounded, but George, who hadn't completely adjusted to his new eyesight and whose aim bordered on the absurd, was struck down by a concise headshot, spewing his brains out from the back of his head. And when Lenny got home, he bragged about his victory and called the battle his own private Ragnarök.

In February, June died. She'd been suffering from cancer, and Lenny visited her every day, and it broke him when she passed. For days she'd refused to eat, her emaciated body shutting down at a rapid rate, her speech slowing, slurred, and finally ceasing altogether. Tubes entered and exited her body at wayward points, prolonging the inevitable. Lenny didn't know what to do and watched his best friend suffer alone with terror and fear flashing in bursts across a barely recognizable face. In her final 10 seconds, she gripped Lenny's arm, and instinctively, Lenny recoiled, and her hand dropped, and she was dead, and Lenny sat in silence, impotent to have helped his friend—his talents all moot, mostly focused on destructive and delirium-inducing ends, as our story shows; he was no miracle worker, a conjuror of cheap tricks even, a limp dick of uselessness when faced with the proper foe: the seemingly infinite indifference of a misbegotten universe, as some with a more negative lens might have characterized it.

He was at an all-time low, and he was unsure what to do next. He felt oddly light and buoyant and broken and shattered, and the mixture was strange, and he didn't know what to do. He left the hospital, and when he realized where he was, it was too late.

He was at the door of the family he'd taken on that strange, cursory Christmas adventure not long before, and they let him in, and he only got a few syllables out, but the woman seemed to understand, and she put her arm around Lenny whose emotions broke free, and tears began to stream down his long and hairy face, and the young boy came up to him and asked him what was wrong and told him it'd be all right and brought him some milk and showed him his toy train, and then he asked Lenny if he'd seen his missing cat, a cat named Meowsers, or Meowson, or something similar to that.

Years and decades and centuries passed by, and Lenny became so profoundly odd and against the times that he could no longer live in the comfort of the civilized world. It had changed significantly; architecture of a terrifying stature grew out of the world's cities; skylines and tunnels and loops and slides and intricately connected pathways between 100-story buildings were the norm, and celestial exploration was mankind's primary focus, even though it only cemented their smallness. It was as if, in the future, man saw his place as a dwarf in the cosmos, and as a means of assimilating, he tried to reduce his stature more and more, to a microscopic size, a vanishing trick; a pious attempt to lend sanctity to space and deify its vastness, to cure man of his pride by flinging him further and further into the extraordinary expanses of the Great Unknown or the Void or, as an old German pessimist might have dubbed the whole affair, a drowning death in the abysses of nothingness.

As the years went on, Lenny became obsessed with the idea of the art of the exit. The proper time to terminate the game, close the curtains, end the ordeal. He wanted to construct the perfect endnote, something shattering and complex that echoed and reverberated off and out into the cosmos. In other words, a triumphant finale, one whose execution Lenny could look forward to with hope and excitement, even though it meant his death, or his end, which should have made him feel sad or worried but actually made him feel energetic and giddy. Lenny: a god who'd lived a long goddamn time, who'd seen the sights and shook the hands of many folk and even bedded down with some beautiful persons along the way, killing and smiling and laughing his way towards an abrupt period at the end of an overlong sentence.

He arrived on Easter Island alone and brought his 9mm pistol with him. The first day there he wrote two small pieces of writing. The first piece goes:

A creative endeavor seems to be nothing more than a vomiting of the soul. A gag reflex spurred on by an involuntary shove by some mechanism operating within the so-called poet. Disgusted and disgruntled, he or she unleashes the fury raging in their guts, splashing the scene with colors of half-digested food and dark-green-to-yellowish-brown bile. People applaud such efforts, puking not being an altogether untalented activity, requiring a certain art of projection and physical robustness.

The second piece was a poem and it went:

The end goal was always the same,
Happiness,
Completion,
Idleness.
Laziness was a slow machine,
Working at a slow pace,
Trying to fit in.
Idleness was the fastest.
Sitting still.
The goal accomplished.
Bang.

On the fourth day, he felt an obscure and veiled emotion somewhat resembling hope, but darker and more brooding, sprinkled with despair, and he didn't know where it came from, but he supposed this was the best he'd get, emotionally speaking, for the task at hand; simply put, the time had come. *"Weren't all endings cheap and abrupt?"* He thought so. To hell with the vanity of an extravagant exit, he'd die like a dog like the rest of them, solidarity with his fellow man, or something like that. So, he stood up on a rock and decided to read his poem or mumble it, since he made the awkward decision of shoving the gun in his mouth, and right before the final line, he'd pull the trigger. A corny exit, but whatever.

Sitting still.
The goal accomplished...

Click.
It was supposed to be a bang, but it ended up being a click, and the gun had jammed, and Lenny still had his head, and he decided that perhaps this was a sign, but really, he rethought his position and said fuck it and was happy to still be intact, and he grabbed his gear and went back to his sanctuary, far in the north, to scribble some more shit and barf his brains out.

Chapter 25: The Diner

Back at the diner, the one we started at, sit many of the guests we've come to know over the course of our varied tale. Look yonder, and you'll see Richard, near the window, and over there, Joyce, sitting alone at a table for two. This is a typical Sunday night crowd. The patrons dig in and mash mounds of beautifully prepared food into the trenches of their gullets, made with love by an elderly, overweight chef by the name of Carmell. She fixes the best chow in the whole state, and people come from far and wide to this eatery off an old forgotten road, to dine at this dimly lit sanctuary branded with neon bulbs.

One of the highest acts of love is the preparation and donation of nourishment for another. This was one of Carmell's favorite sayings; she said she got it from the Bible, but no one ever found any proof of this, although no one at the diner knew the Bible all that well, and they asked her if maybe it was from another religious text or book or pamphlet, but she said no, it was definitely the Bible.

Over the years, the regulars tired of this hackneyed saying, but Carmell didn't give a damn and continued to use it whenever she pleased. She said that it was true and that truth was timeless, and because of this, it needed to be heard, and the more often, the better. But then someone asked her about clichés and about beating words into the ground and the flux-like nature of language, and she got all flustered and changed the topic. A few nights later, a trucker heading east on a long coastal drive stopped in, and after hearing the above-mentioned quote, he told her that he'd never forget those lovely and inspiring words about love and food and all that stuff, and he said he loved her homespun wisdom and her shepherd's pie, and an hour later, back on the road, he'd forgotten the words entirely, but he wished he'd ordered another helping of her hearty and flavorsome victuals to go.

That night, Richard ordered his usual, a pan-fried steak with onions and peppers served with a mushroom sauce and fries. It arrived piping hot and was delicious as hell, and Richard salivated and drooled all over his plate before he bit into the bloody and perfectly seasoned meat. When Carmell came over to see how he was enjoying his food, he growled at her, half-crazed and partly in appreciation, and she smiled at Richard, although she was beginning to believe that something might be wrong with him, particularly with his head—or with his mind, which she thought of as one and the same. When he finished, he went up to the till and paid and thanked her, this time using proper English, and she said you're welcome, and he retorted with a "see you soon," and then he exited the diner and went out into the cold, baying night.

**

Although the diner could be described as a clean and hospitable place, it nonetheless has a few vermin hidden away among its nooks and crannies, as most, if not all, places do; out of sight and out of mind, but there all the same. The diner's vermin are mostly made up of spiders and ants and sometimes a few mice—although if Carmell sees a mouse, things go on lockdown, and the whole restaurant is halted; a sign is placed at the door (temporarily closed for renovations or culinary experimentations), and machinations of doom are drawn up as Carmell and an exterminator friend go to work with an assortment of poisons and traps and meat cleavers. They don the garb of killers, and once the threat is eradicated, the diner returns to its former bearings, none except Carmell and the exterminator and the dead rodents any wiser.

There's a house about a mile from the diner; it, too, lies hidden or off the beaten path, mostly unbothered by the outside world. Only once a month does the house come alive. On this night, usually the first Saturday of each month, cars of all makes and models drive up, typically around 11 p.m., and large men in suits stand at its gate, halting traffic before allowing certain ones entry. Some vehicles are rusty and bottomed out, while others arrive in sheen metallic stallions of highbrow engineering. It is difficult to guess which cars will gain entry based on their appearances alone, aristocratic rides are as frequently denied as the poor misbegotten ones, and one can only suppose that it's the drivers lurking beneath who are really the cause of entry or dismissal. One can also suppose that the guests all come from various socioeconomic backgrounds, but this could be a trick, and maybe the vehicles are like masks, to camouflage or throw people off the scent, as unsuspecting onlookers watch menial and decrepit machines pass them by with geniuses or madmen or murderers or lovers at the wheel, rich in funds and madness; they are the ghosts dialing in the commands and passing before a disinterested public gaze. At bottom, one can at least suppose that the pool is varied and that each guest at the party plays some role within its mysterious festivities.

Two hicks from a nearby town hear about the party and decide to crash it. Aware that simply hopping the gate won't do—presumably security is tight everywhere, but tightest at the central opening—they decide to go the long way around, entry via another roadway off behind the house. They will sneak in and map out a quiet and unassuming route. They heard that the party is a giant orgy full of big-breasted goddesses and less-than-virile old men. If they cannot join in, they will at least be privy to a good show. They decide to dress in dark tones, and each has a flashlight, a phone, a Swiss Army knife, and a .22 tucked into his underpants in case events go haywire or astray.

The first bit of their plan goes off without a hitch, and they park their truck, hiding it in a field on the opposite side of the road. They dig a hole by the fence, just big enough for them to squeeze through; each is fairly skinny, but only one is nimble; the other is relatively stiff from years of routinized manual labor, the same movement done over and over again, and his friend has to push and prod him to get him through—success— and only a slightly pulled hip flexor to boot; the men hobble off into the night through dense brush and marshlands, striving towards their ominous destination.

The thicket seems to go on for some time, and neither one can see any singular source of light to lend them some navigational point of interest. They begin to hear noises that are not of their making, and Rudy (the stiff one) notices that he's lost his pal (Jake), and he's now alone in a potentially hostile environment; he's nervous and begins to sweat, but before he can call out his pal's name and withdraw his firearm, he is whacked on the head by an unknown assailant and darkness envelops him.

When Rudy comes to, he's in a house, "the house" probably, perhaps fate has accelerated his plans and delivered him to his destination in the quickest possible manner, a straight line between two adjacent points, journeyed in darkness under the cover of his sublime unconscious. He looks around and notices that he's tied to a chair, rather tightly too, and his clothes are gone, missing in fact, and someone has dressed him like an 18th-century aristocrat, wig and all, and makeup too. He can see his reflection off in a distant mirror; he looks ridiculous and wishes he had his camo coat back and feels degraded, less so because of his capture and more so because of his style. He has a decent vantage point from the chair, and he sees that the party is in full swing. It doesn't appear to have much in the way of sexual content, not out in the open at least, and he notices that each participant seems to be dressed in an obnoxious costume tied to no singular period, purpose, or theme, at least none that Rudy can determine, as anachronisms abound, and at best, it looks to him like some surrealist ball hosted by the Rothschilds, but less glamorous and more hokey.

No one seems to be paying him much attention; it's as if some captive occupant in antiquated regalia were all part of the show.

A man dressed from the same epoch comes by and addresses him. He calls him a naughty boy and wags a gloved finger in an overly theatrical fashion, and with the help of a few of the large, hulking men, they lift Rudy and the chair and take him to the veranda where a man with an elephant gun—dressed as a white hunter from the dawn of the 20th century—nods politely and loads his weapon.

The surrounding landscape is well groomed, and a clearing of about 100 yards of well-cut grass separates the forest from the house. Rudy is told to pay close attention, and the white hunter yells, "Ready," and far off in the distance, galloping in their direction, a wild thing emerges from the forest, running towards the veranda with dogs chomping at its feet. As the bipedal beast gets closer, he notices that it's not an animal— well, technically it is—but it's a human animal, dressed as a beast, in a bear costume, but with the mask of a pig, or something that resembles a pig, with a prominent and ugly snout. As it gets nearer, chased by the rabid canines, the great white hunter levels his rifle, and the aristocrat says, "Take aim!" and the hunter sets his sights on the costumed creature right before the firing command is issued, and a booming commotion rattles the walls and the chinaware, and the party stops... momentarily. Then, as if the intrusion had been expected, the frivolities continue; unconcerned by the bang, the music plays on (a nocturne, no doubt), and the beast is down, a giant hole, or holes, where its torso once was—a downed and disfigured simian—and all present on the veranda remove their hats or wigs or whatever was stationed atop their mighty heads, a show of respect, more theatrics! And the aristocrat makes a toast, "To Jake, the bravest bear of them all." And the first thought running through Rudy's mind is, "But why the snout?"

Rudy and Jake are never heard from again, and the nearby town cares little about their disappearance. They weren't the most popular lads, and people chat about their case mostly because of its unsolved nature, mysteries always adding an air of intrigue to the conversation, even when dressed with uninteresting players. The diner seems to have succumbed to the allure of the gossip, not surprising since the incident occurred right next door, although no one here technically knows that, or maybe they do... but they aren't telling anyone, at least not here; and Joyce and Tom discuss possible theories as varied as UFO abduction and extended Middle Eastern vacations, and no one seems to have even the foggiest clue about what happened to those two schmucks. Weeks go by, and the diner is still abuzz with speculation; it is safe to assume that the shadow of the event lingers over the proximal area in which the vile act occurred. The diner can't help but pick up on the dark vibes emanating from its closest neighbor. As other parts of town seem to have moved on from the event without a hitch, the diner remains fixed under the spell of Rudy and Jake's unexplained disappearance or—as the diner's patrons have come to nickname the puzzling affair—Rake's hiatus or, more aptly put, Rake's death or, better yet, the elephant's enigma.

The root of genius and the root of evil both extend from the unbearable price of simplicity, or the quickest route between two points can sometimes make you go crazy or mad or succeed beyond your wildest and most unrealistic dreams.

***

Gwen stopped off at the diner with her father, and they sat at their usual spot. The fourteen-year-old Gwen aimed her sights at the special, a Salisbury steak with homemade gravy served with a Caesar salad, while her father skipped dinner and stuck to cigarettes, coffee, and a slice of apple pie. Their presence in the diner was warm and amicable, if not somewhat downbeat.

They had an affectionate way of slowing down the rhythm of wherever they were. Gwen's father once said that calmness and happiness were synonyms and became more and more interchangeable as one got older. He looked on disinterestedly at many of his friends' lives whose midlife crises had them parachuting out of planes and bedding down with beautiful, but mostly unstable, twenty-somethings. This tactic of spiritual rejuvenation through intensity seemed ill-conceived according to Gwen's father; not a good long-term strategy, he thought. Not that he didn't enjoy the company of young, beautiful women, but unlike some of his friends—whose tactics were centered on glorifying the young damsels with gifts and trips and the like, playing an offensive, high-energy game, so to speak, or in other words, using money and attention to keep the hook constantly baited—he preferred to wait quietly and let them acclimate to his rhythm, and if they found his assured and mature tone appealing, then he'd approach, but first he needed some sign or gesture, not necessarily a submissive one, but one of agreement. As if through his earnest, if not lackadaisical, demeanor, he could put forth a contract, setting the pace, and if they were interested, they'd pare down their speed, find his rhythm, join his rank.

He knew that the slower tempo he offered was in rare supply among young men, or men in general nowadays, and its appeal, although not widespread, still beckoned a certain type. It wasn't an approach that garnered the most results, but it required less effort to sustain—almost none in fact—and usually brought the best and most rewarding experiences emotionally and sexually, although patience was often, if not always, required. And he referred to this stratagem as the tortoise tactic.

Gwen saw George sitting with his wife at another table, and she went over to say hi. George was one of her high school teachers. He taught English, and she found his teaching style unorthodox and effective. He'd often hold discussions on topics unrelated to the syllabus. Although he did his best to get them through the basic scope of their government-regulated curriculum, he used a good chunk of class time to go over world events, talk about movies and the media and whatever else was rippling through the modern psyche. He talked about calamities and anxieties and helped his class frame the world in a way that would hopefully ease their growing tension. He cared less about helping them form a general and hardened perspective, believing that the indoctrination of a firm point of view always came across as ham-fisted, and potentially dangerous, especially when concerned with the pliable minds of youth. He was trying to reestablish equilibrium with his students whereby their minds could go about performing their natural processes—a psyche properly managing and amalgamating and destroying and reconfiguring and shifting and absorbing and discarding and shitting and all the other stuff each and every mind was forced to do, day in and day out. He simply wanted to impart to them the intuitive gift of digestion by revealing to them how to do something they didn't know they already knew how to do. Gwen—not entirely grasping the scope of the concepts, or what it was she was actually learning from George's tangential chats (he never explained his goals overtly)—was nonetheless content to be in his class and looked forward to his lessons; they energized her and compelled her towards some innate hidden drive, and years later, when she thought back to them, she'd smile, and believe him to be a rarity among the world, a genuine and gifted teacher.

***

The skull of a man is found on a hiking trail not far from the diner by a fellow named Glen and a dog named Poe. They were out, minding their business, when Poe sniffed her way off the path and into the bush and made her macabre discovery. Glen called the police right away, and through forensic analysis, the cops were able to deduce that the bones were that of Rudy Sinclair—known thief, peeping Tom, and associate of another missing resident, Jake Leboeuf.

***

The old man and the kid enter the diner, and Carmell says hi, but only the kid responds. The old man is making a beeline towards his spot, and the kid trails, unhurried. Once their order is taken, coffee and chocolate milk, the old man says to the kid, "Christ in a fart tavern, does it smell like a rank turd in here!" The kid is embarrassed by the old man's outburst but knows that there's no point in making his feelings known. The old man is without remorse. He sees these moments as learning opportunities for the kid—to break through the barriers of socially constructed stigmas, displace the markers of shame and decency, shake up the established order. The kid sees it differently. They order hamburgers, and the old man asks the kid how school is going, and midway through his answer, the old man interrupts, veering the conversation in an altogether different direction, one more suited to his current temperament, and the kid is left hanging with a half-eaten hamburger on his plate and an egotistical old man blinking back at him.

After they eat, the old man and the kid sit for a while, shooting the shit, and the kid asks the old man what he thinks about Rudy Sinclair's bones turning up the way they did, and the old man scoffs; he says that he probably had it coming, not necessarily the death part, but certainly the part about being chucked in the woods, right on his ass, to rot and disappear and then reappear. The kid doesn't know what to make of this response, so he asks the old man what he thinks might have happened, and the old man says, "I know what happened. Those assholes up in that house over yonder ate him."

This answer precipitates more questions, like who are these people, and what house is he referring to? The kid has never seen any house like that around here, or he's seen houses, but he can't distinguish "the house," the one that eats its guests and discards their remains out in the bush. But the old man tires of the topic quickly and starts complaining about the state of modern television commercials and the new light bulbs Carmell has installed in the diner, which to him are malfunctioning, at least in respect to their color temperature, which he assumes to be roughly 850K off from their proper range. The kid gives up and orders a Cherry Coke, a consolation prize in lieu of the old man's answer to who murdered, ate, and discarded Rudy Sinclair. But it never occurs to the kid to ask the old man how he knows, which is probably the more interesting question.

Weeks go by, and once again, it's the first Saturday of the month. The house is alive, and the masquerade rejoices in her former glories; vehicles of various standings are parked out on the field near the front entrance. It's 1 a.m., and the party is running at full tilt. It's December, and as a special nod to the final party of the year, the members dial back their usual costumed personas and come as they appear out there, in the regular world; and each guest, upon entering, is given a mask, a clear translucent thing that distorts the wearer's face while not entirely concealing their identity. Gwen is here, her father too. Carmell is carving some unknown meat under a heat lamp, and George, the high school teacher, is lecturing the old man, who, against his better judgment, has brought the kid with him for the first time. George's lecture centers on some political upheaval out in northern Sudan, and the old man, as per usual, is only half listening, happy the mask distorts his features just enough to conceal his grimace. Richard, out on the veranda, pontificates openly about God knows what, and his lecture quickly nosedives into incomprehension as he growls and tongue clacks at the surrounding guests who disperse to other areas of the house in droves.

Joyce enters the scene, the Thin Pink Duke as she's often referred to here. Her elegance on full display. A long red dress dances along the contours of her flesh and accentuates her voluptuous underbelly. She begins the main event by tapping her staff 3 times against the marble floor and leads the guests into another room where—veiled under a tarp—an English professor waits, tied and gagged and nervous, as he should be, particularly if he has any idea as to what awaits him further on down the line.

The professor was chosen for various reasons to act as the sacrificial cow this evening. First off, he has written a book, Nietzschean in nature, and its global appeal has wreaked havoc on the world order, giving bad people good ideas, or debasing good ideas to make them palatable for bad people, or seasoning them just so, so that their main properties, or points, are distorted and diminished enough to land among the general populace. Although this isn't his primary sin, as anyone who's created anything can tell you, once it lands in the world's hands, it no longer belongs to you, the artist, and in much the same way, your culpability regarding its impact is rendered rather moot. Even trying to sway or direct the narrative often has adverse and unforeseen and, more often than not, negligible consequences. So, this accusation is generally unfounded, and most of the partygoers see it as a fabricated charge to hold up the appearance of guilt when, in fact, it's because no one really likes the professor. There's one artist here in particular who disagrees so wholeheartedly with this charge that he wishes to set the man free, maybe just with a warning, or keep him on as a groundskeeper, or as part of the custodial staff. He argues that all any artist can do is get the work done and remain present, to the best of their ability, while doing so. Anything beyond that is outside his or her control including talent and all its accompanying flourishes. Nonetheless, the English professor's guilt was proven incontrovertible by the second charge, which no one really knew the facts about, but Joyce reassured them and alluded to its atrocious nature, and she made hints that the professor had a predilection for underage girls. The two charges were enough to condemn the man, although very little evidence was brought forth to verify the claims, apart from rumors and hearsay and Joyce's condemnations, but like I said, no one really liked him, so the deck was already stacked against him from the beginning.

Gwen was given the honor and handed a chef's knife, and they took the gag from the professor's mouth, and he said, "All the children are insane." And she replied, "50% of opinions are absolute horseshit—including most of my own." He was slightly perplexed by this reply, but the knife slid into his guts a fraction of a second later, and his attention was on the wound and not the words, and being the good butcher that she was, Gwen got some vital organs on her second penetrating thrust, and the professor was down for the count shortly thereafter.

Driving home around 5:30 a.m., the old man and the kid, stuffed on chow, drive quietly along empty, darkened roads. The kid asks the old man how long these events or vigils or offerings have been going on, and the old man replies, "Since the dawn of man, my boy. And they'll continue to go on under the guise of one costume or another. We are like lost dogs vilified by the urge to purge, and until life as we know it ceases to be, and the inanimate and soulless reclaim the throne upon which the universe was built, the mad and the masked shall have their dance and frolic and play and abuse the day." The kid was surprised by the old man's wickedness, but for some reason, he wanted to hug him and found his evil and baseness sublime and endearing, and even a little comforting somehow. But all this passed as the old man went on another tangent and started talking about poorly divided subdivisions out in a new housing development east of town, and all his murderous mystique fell to the wayside, and he regained his normal and deaf and offending demeanor, a counterfeit only playing at the sublime, a man less than the sum of his crimes.

Chapter 26: The Old Man and the Kid

The old man and the kid decided to hit the road after the events described in the previous chapter. They set out on a cross-country odyssey, through plains and mountain ranges, and set their sights on a desert destination in the heart of a no-man's-land. The trip started well enough, with the old man happy to depart his neck of the woods, steer clear of his usual trappings for a while, trade it all in for a rough-and-tumble adventure, just him and the kid and the highways and byways of the Americas; but his newfound optimism was short-lived, and upheaval and chaos were baring their fangs in wait, right around the corner, at the first rest stop, actually, not 2 hours from where they had begun, just due south; and the old man, having an old and worn bladder, had to relieve himself rather badly and rather suddenly, and he pulled over at the nearest rest stop and made a hasty decision to piss on the outside wall of the rest stop, as opposed to going inside the rest stop, which was a small 250-square-foot shop selling trinkets and maps and potato chips, since the one bathroom inside had an "out of service" sign hanging on the door. And the attendant at the rest stop spotted the old man mid-piss, but in reality, he heard him first, as the old man let out a loud and thunderous fart, and even giggled shortly thereafter, bringing unwanted attention his way, and the attendant came running over, all threatening-like, waving his disgruntled and hairy fists, demanding that the old man stop, discontinue his flow, immediate cessation of all activity. But the old man did no such thing, knowing from experience the pain of an abrupt mid-stream pause, he continued, cock and balls on display, still pissing, and he faced the attendant and began to threaten him, describing the torrent of fury coming his way if he didn't back off, leave him be, allow him the courtesy and privacy of finishing up his business unbothered, just an old man and his pecker, out in the open air, whizzing on a wall. The kid was still in the truck during all this and prayed to the heavens above that he wouldn't have to intercede, but the old man pointed over in his direction, and he knew he'd have to get out and go over there, pacify the situation as best he could. The attendant by now had lost most, if not all, of his restraint and poise, and the odds of fisticuffs were multiplying tenfold. The kid knew that the old man wouldn't back down and that a light breeze, let alone the wrath of an angered and husky rest stop attendant, could easily blow him over, or break him in two, or squash him like a millipede. The kid stepped towards the attendant, ready to prostrate for the man's forgiveness on behalf of the old crazy pisser, just as the old man resorted to his final knavish trick, directing his stream at his antagonist, thrusting the pair headlong towards a violent confrontation, the final degrading straw; and just like that, with the gleam of piss on his fat, pockmarked shins, the attendant widened his stance and threw a wild punch and laid that old motherfucker out with a single brutalizing blow; and then the kid entered the fight, made an effort to hold his own, avenge his partner, dance toe-to-toe with the beast, but he lasted no more than a few brief seconds before receiving a shot to the chops and another to his kidneys, and he tumbled over, defeated, and the pair of weaklings remained prone and earthbound, in a puddle of piss, for the better part of an hour before they could muster enough strength to return to the truck and drive off.

The old man's diarrhea paints a stupendous composition on the porcelain bowl. It is a masterpiece of abstract expressionism if one is able to frame it that way, disengage it from its surroundings, look closely and discover the intense and detailed beauty lurking beneath its base and humble beginnings. Many works of art are marred by these origins, identities formed at their conception, a shadow hanging over their birth, an inheritance coiled to their creation, and these works, generally those represented in non-narrative mediums—e.g., painting and the like—seem to be the most susceptible to these biographical prejudices. Narrative in this context having little to do with storytelling and more to do with sequence and order. For example, in books, words follow words. In films, images follow images. In music, notes follow notes. Narrative in rhythm, sculpted in succession, capable of engaging the viewer or listener with flashes of something new, revealing itself bit by bit, led by tones and symbols, a dance through time, hypnotic and, most importantly, manipulative—whereas painting, whose power to render shock and emotional ecstasies suddenly and with great force, falls victim to its own severity, its completeness taken in all at once; it demands mystery because of its brevity, and through its wholeness, the world, more often than not, feels the need to feed it additional information, expand its narrative, diversify its canon. Let's say that the shit-splattered masterpiece, whose lines and colors rival those of a Jackson Pollock painting—the shitter, in this case, the old man, whose diet and digestive maladies espouse a colorful kind of bowel movement not normally seen in younger and healthier folk— is photographed and blown up and printed and displayed in a gallery. The guests swoon over its technical prowess and sharp, aggressive streaks, unaware of its fecal properties, but then the knowledge is spilled, its pedigree known, and the guests learn of its inherent shittiness, and the painting, or (as it has now become) the photograph, becomes submissive to this knowledge, tied to it irrevocably, very rarely, if ever, able to surmount this aspect of its story, which could propel it to success or diminish it to worthlessness, at least financially, which is the heart of the art world, a business of chicness, and the composition, so naturally created—an explosion of inner turmoil—is chained to its founding truth, at least in the public's eye, but maybe not the artist's (the old man), who flushes his masterwork down the pipe, unaware of its sickening beauty, as he hasn't even looked at it, completely disinterested, not to mention the fact that he can only see out of one eye, the other, swollen shut, battered by a fat asshole with no sense of humor, and he looks in the mirror, and he washes his hands, but he forgets to dry them.

The pair continues their voyage, and one night, stopped at a motel, they meet a fellow traveler, a Black man who proclaims himself a prophet. A genuine mystic with oneiric visions, he sees crumpled and poorly compiled versions of the future, usually somewhat out of whack or order, in strange Technicolor pop. He tells the old man and the kid that he saw them two nights ago, in a dream, only the kid was a caterpillar—a real fat son of a gun—and the old man was a spider (old and slow but venomous all the same), and they lived together in a small clearing right in the middle of an ornery-looking farmer's field, but then he corrected himself and said it was in a garden and not a field. He told them they spent most of their days—in the dream at least—going on adventures, helping and betraying friends and foes alike, eating neighbors and plants and other small critters, lounging on various botanical specimens and generally living rather lovely and high-spirited lives. But then he warned them, told them a dark cloud and a threatening force grew over their garden and was approaching as they spoke and that they must prepare; the final boss was coming, a real mean SOB, and in this dream, it was personified as a yellowish figure, with swaths of red and brown stretched over its infected skin; it had slits for eyes and nostrils, and the only prominent feature on its head was a large mouth chock-full of crowded teeth. Shit, thought the kid, I really hope this old prescient tiger is wrong about this. The old man paid the prophet no mind and went back to his room and tried to watch a stuttering preacher on TV but fell asleep at the first commercial break, and he dreamed he was in some sort of marshland, the moon guiding his way, and he was trying—rather unsuccessfully—to locate a stone staircase, leading him down to the base of an empty well, where a light (or a dark light as he figured it was) was waiting, eager to meet his eyes and impart to him its vast and terrifying secret. After 8 hours of this, he woke up, wet and perspiring; he muttered, "Ah, fuck," and realized he'd pissed himself yet again.

The next day, they hit the road early and took their breakfast to go. The kid had also had an odd dream, perhaps
influenced by the predictions and mutterings of the self-
proclaimed prophet, perhaps not, and when he tried to tell the
old man about it, the old man interrupted him and told him
that he'd had enough of listening to dreams, and that if he was
worried or disturbed by his nocturnal imaginings, he should
take it up with his subconscious or his psyche or whatever part
of him was responsible for the movie playing in his head in
those odd and late hours—the so-called projectionist inside,
switching reels in the most obtuse and exhilarating ways,
devising a montage of what would most disturb or fascinate or
emotionally resonate with the dreamer, essentially cheating
as they were privy to all the potent and repressed elixirs
lurking in the mind's deepest recesses, and they knew
exactly what would most easily manipulate the viewer, or the
dreamer, because they too were the dreamer—a dual role—
creating a fiction for themselves, by themselves; a creator and
spectator played concurrently and without repose.

They passed a small town and drove down its main street.
Little shops appeared, and they saw a hamburger stand and
parked their truck and walked over. Famished as they were,
they each ordered 3 hamburgers from a small woman behind
a sliding glass window. She did not smile and wiggled her lips
between sentences, and the old man, whose eyesight had
deteriorated rather steadily over the past few years—not to
mention his most recent shenanigans, which, for now, had left
him with only one properly performing eye—could still spot
ample bushels of hair fluttering on the hamburger mistress's
manic upper lip. Despite all his visual limitations, her
mustache entered his purview. He wondered if she was the
chef too, a multitalented employee, and sure enough, once

they'd placed their orders and paid the bill, the madam hopped off her stool (she being far shorter than the old man had even supposed), and she went about her business, slapping meat patties on the grill, shaving onions and lettuce and tomatoes and dressing the buns with butter and some mysterious sauce that was later thought to be BBQ sauce (both sweet and smoky), and they each gave two big, enthusiastic thumbs-up to the hamburger stand and the little chef with her despondent facial hair and her unwavering commitment to satisfying and delicious all-American fare.

5 days had elapsed since they'd set out on their trip, and they were only now entering their first big city. They had remained off the main arteries and used little-known gravel roads as much as they could, both for scenic value and to remain off the radar, but whose radar were they hiding from? It was a big southern city with skyscrapers and turnpikes and traffic and concrete paraphernalia displaying the richness and vastness of a colony gone off its rocker with megalomania and progress. The need to build and create and push and prod superseding all others, pacifying the crowd's need to remain agog and stimulated—movement above reflection, speed above silence; and the kid was happy to be back in the civilized world, and the radio played a pop song with a refined, repetitive chorus and a blazing electronic beat. The old man muttered to himself and parked in an underground parking garage, and he and the kid entered a large, towering edifice whose shape was cylindrical and phallic.

They took the elevator up to the 12th floor and then took the stairs down to another floor. The kid was told to wait outside with a receptionist who smiled at him in a fashion unbefitting to social norms. When the old man exited the office, he held a map and wore an appeased but worried look. He took the boy's arm as if to hurry him, even though he was the slow one, and the pair went back up the stairs and took the elevator down, this time, to a subbasement, and when the doors opened, it appeared to be a giant warehouse, or stockroom, with hundreds of rows of boxes and labeled goods aligning this subterranean storage chamber. The old man went off on his own again, and the kid was told to wait, lucky for him, a man in a forklift was displaying virtuoso skill, adding and subtracting items to his forks with speed and dexterity, balancing the dangerous loads with ease and barreling down the tight corridors with precision and grace, all the while puffing away on a cigarette—one after another—his face bored and aloof.

After they finished in the city and grabbed some food, they returned to the rural roads and secondary highways, the country's system of nerves extending across its greater whole, allowing for a large possibility of routes to get from point A to wherever the hell point B was. They entered another small town around midnight, and the old man told the kid they needed to see a friend. They stopped at an office with a red neon sign stuck against a sullied window, blinds closed. The sign displayed the contours of an alligator with no accompanying words. The streets were deserted, and the kid spotted a tumbleweed down the way, a cinematographic stereotype furnishing them tone. The old man walked in without knocking, and inside, a fat man sat at a desk, puffing away at a cigar under a lone lamp. The man with the cigar pointed at a desk in the corner, and the old man sat down at it. It faced a clock on an adjacent wall, and the desk had a towel draped over it, concealing some object beneath. The old man removed the towel, and the kid—who remained near the door—saw a meat cleaver lying there. The old man looked at the cigar-smoking man who pointed to a blackboard behind his head; it was empty except for a dollar sign drawn in large font near its center. The old man nodded and, without a word, extended his left arm across the table and raised the meat cleaver and brought it down, severing his hand from his wrist with one strike. He screamed, fell over, gasped for a few seconds, then passed out, blood spurting everywhere. The cigar-smoking man got up, grabbed something from under his desk, a bucket, poured some liquid into it and then dropped his cigar in. Flames erupted but subdued themselves rather quickly; he crouched near the old man and took his severed hand and placed it inside the flaming bucket and began muttering some gibberish. The kid's shock somewhat dissipating at this point, he ran over to the old man and tried to help, but how? And the cigar-smoking man shushed him and kept yammering away in some unknown tongue, bucket ablaze, severed hand within, and then, a minute or two later, the cigar-smoking man, having ceased his mutterings, grabbed the meat cleaver and placed its blade in the bucket; it emerged, scorching hot, and he placed the blade against the old man's wrist, sealing the wound, and the kid couldn't help but think of the hamburger stand from a few days before, the odor in the office comparable, and he salivated briefly, wondering if there wasn't one such restaurant close by. Then he reproached himself for the thought, and he and the cigar-smoking man carried the old man to the truck, and without a word, the cigar-smoking man returned to his office and extinguished the neon alligator out front.

The kid wanted to take the old man to a hospital, but after driving through the hamlet, he was unable to find any building resembling one whose function catered to medical emergencies. He drove a little ways outside of town and parked just off the road in a grass field and waited for the old man to wake up, which he did, not long after 7 a.m., and he looked at his wrist and moved his right hand over where, 24 hours prior, another almost identical appendage had been secured. He told the kid to go to the bed of the truck and open the toolkit and grab the whiskey bottle inside. The kid did as he was told, and he gave the bottle to the old man who took a big drink before emptying some of its contents over his wound; he winced and then passed out for another 4 hours.

***

The blood from the old man's wound is soaked up by a flyer lying crumpled up on the floor. The flyer was placed beneath the windshield wiper by some passerby and carelessly tossed in the truck by the old man a few days before. The blood has developed into a strange pattern, curling and crafting a run across the breadth of the flyer, splitting and drying and remerging from various points. Words unobscured by the blood's random trajectory are chosen and written down, and a collection of sentences are composed using only those 50-plus words—a shamanistic experiment in forfeiture, to give up control and distance oneself from the rational rules of writing. One of the sentences developed using this method reads, "All the truth in the world adds up to 1 big lie." Another goes, "All players are saints, villains, and cannibals." And still another, "Each path in the abattoir is a forking one." The flyer is from a pizzeria called Little Jim's, and a cartoon ninja is printed on its front page, and it sells pizzas with names like "The Flying Saucer Deluxe" (double pepperoni with Alfredo sauce and marinara sauce) and "Hong Kong Master vs. Hawaiian

Commando" (pineapple and shredded beef marinated in ginger sauce with ham and arugula). The experiment is deemed a success, and the old man's dripping stump is hailed as a master wordsmith, cracking the code and revitalizing the written word by way of optimal and inspired choices—although he is completely unaware of this, broken and beaten and mutilated as he is. And the omniscient gods peering into the old man's world giggle at the flyer lying dormant and useless, secrets no mind shall ever perceive, at least not by way of these two derelicts and their bloodstained opus; and the old man wakes up and mutters a few nonsensical words to the kid before telling him to get the map on top of the dashboard and drive to the spot marked by an asterisk. And the kid does just that, and the two vile poets are barreling down the road, closing in on their final destination.

The kid follows the map, and they end up on the outskirts of some town, at a diner, in the desert, not completely different from the one they used to frequent near their hometown. This one, however, is long and seems to be modeled after a caboose of sorts, and he wakes the old man up who has duct-taped a plastic bag around his stump and changed his coat for one less grubby and also less blood-stained. They enter the diner and find a seat. The kid asks the old man why they are here. Why have they traveled the length of the country to arrive at this specific place? The old man fumbles with his coat and checks his shirt pocket, making sure whatever's in there remains so, and the kid sits waiting in anticipation of an answer that doesn't arrive. The old man grumbles some words and gets up and makes his way to the bathroom, and out of earshot from the dining patrons, the old man sits discarding dislodged stools from his bowels. He pulls a felt-tip pen from his shirt pocket and draws four intersecting lines and writes the word "asshole" underneath. Next to it, he draws an identical image and writes the word "universe." He exits the bathroom without washing his hand and stares absentmindedly at the crowd near the booth by the window. The kid notices the old man's eyes: they've changed, displaying a new emotion, an emotion that resembles fear or nervousness, and this confuses the kid, who begins to fall victim to his own brand of terror, creeping in from who knows where, flooding the room, and the kid looks around, out the window, and the wind seems to be out of its mind, spinning and circling and catapulting debris with violent aplomb and threatening gravitas, and the lights in the already dim diner extinguish, except for the lights above the duo, but none of the other patrons or waitresses or cooks seem to have noticed the disruptions or the darkness or the wind, just the kid and the old man. And the old man says, "This is it. This is the one we are here to meet. Her diction is different than ours, and her evil and vileness are manifold. We are no longer where we once were, and now we must exit in order to enter. She has invited us in, but I do not know her intentions. I'm sorry, kid." And the old man stood up and clicked his heels 3 times and took the kid's arm, and the pair proceeded to the door, and the kid asked why he too had to face this thing or this beast or this ridiculous god, and the old man said because of what he was and what they were, and the kid asked what that was, and the old man replied, "Beasts and detectives with savage bents and apocryphal tastes. Our destiny is to be doomed, and our doom is our destiny. Let us step out and face our unknown; she waits eagerly to greet us. Let us see what our destiny has in store, whether it be our end or our beginning. Let our curiosity be our downfall." And with these words, the old man opened the exit door and stepped out with the kid into the abysmal blackness, greeted by screaming winds. And the savage detectives glimpsed their fate and were heard from no more.